I0629724

Spade House

Publications

Copyright © 2007 by Rees Porcari
Cover art Copyright © 2007 by William Rees

This book is a work of fiction. Names,
characters, places and incidents are
products of the author's imagination or are
used fictitiously. Any resemblance to actual
events or locales or persons, dead or alive,
is entirely coincidental.

No part of this book may be reproduced in
any form, written or electronically, without
the expressed written consent of the author.

ISBN: 978-0-6151-4778-9

The Ace of Sp♠des

Expect the unexpected.
Trust no one.

Rees Porcari

I would like to dedicate this book to my family. Thank you for helping me with support and criticism along the way. I would like to thank the teachers, past and present, that furthered my education for some of the content in this book, and for helping me learn the "proper" grammar rules. I would like to give a special thanks to my Uncle Will for designing the cover, and to Angela Hooper, who assisted in the editing process. Thank you all.
Rees James Porcari.

Fact: There is one murder approximately
every 33.9 minutes

Fact: Approximately 15,505.2 murders are
committed annually

Stabbing is thought to be the most
personal MO

Part One:
Logan and Ann

No ear can hear nor tongue can tell the
     tortures of the inward hell.
                              -Lord Byron

1

A Dark and Stormy Night

Logan sat by his window and watched the storm. There were two bolts of lightning followed by a monstrous crack of thunder. The storm had been going on for hours now. The streets were starting to fill with murky water; it was coming out of the overflowing drain pipes. There were another two bolts and a monstrous crash of thunder.

When the next bolt of lightning came, Logan counted the seconds until the thunder.

"One one thousand..."

"Two one thousand..."

"Three one..."

Logan was cut off by the thunder.

"Half a mile away," he said to himself.

Logan looked further outside, every house on the street was black, there was nothing to do and it was getting late. The only house that had a light on was his three story on the corner. It was brick and had a very nice front porch. It was white with carved rails and posts. The posts were about nine feet tall, and resembled the poles of the White House; the rails followed same design. Logan and his fiancée, Ann, had moved in two weeks ago. They were finally almost done unpacking; all that was left was the pictures. They couldn't wait till after the wedding so they could show their

families their new house. At his house the dogs
were on the couch whimpering.

Logan looked at the dogs, chuckled, and
said his favorite saying "Stupid no good dogs."
If it wasn't for Ann, Logan would have gotten
rid of them long ago, heck he wouldn't even
have gotten them. The dogs were both shiatsus.
One was overweight, she had dark brown, white,
and black hair. The other was very small, less
than ten pounds with light brown hair. He heard
the sound of nails clicking on the wood floors,
his other dog walked in. This was his favorite
dog. She was a beautiful lab/shepherd mix with
a shining black coat. It was Logan's dog even
before he met Ann.

There was another flash of lightning.
"One one thousand."
"Two..."

He had no chance to finish; the thunder
that interrupted him shook the entire house. At
this the little dogs yelped and jumped towards
Logan. "No, No." He put them on the ground.
"Get off."

They went in the corner and laid down
beside each other.

"Stupid no good dogs," he said again.
Logan would never say this in front of Ann, she
would kill him. He went to the kitchen and got
some Lays baked potato chips and a Bud Light.
He needed to lose a few pounds by next month so
he could fit his tux for his and Ann's wedding.
They were going to the Bahamas tomorrow. Ann
wanted to celebrate the honeymoon first, and
then get married under a beautiful Bahamian
sunset. Logan had no problem with it; he was
looking forward to the honeymoon, *very* much.
After it was over, he could go back to regular
chips and beer.

Then it hit him, he had forgotten to have
their mail held.

"Shit," he said aloud. He already had to get up early to drop the dogs off at the vet, and now he had to stop at the post office. He had no choice though, he needed his mail held; five weeks was too long.

When Logan got back in the living room, he sat down in his new Lay-Z Boy recliner, and turned on the TV; he switched to channel three and turned on his DVD player.

"Ah," Logan said aloud. He just remembered that Ann had stopped on her way to work. The mail was fine.

He was going to watch part of his favorite scary/parody movie trilogy, *Scream*, on a special edition DVD box set. He was going to wait for Ann to start the first *Scream*, but she called about an hour ago and told him that the storm was getting *really* bad and would only be getting worse. She would come home as soon as it died down a little, so he could go ahead and start the first movie. A few minutes into the first *Scream*, right before it started to get good, the phone started to ring.

"Oh for the love of God," Logan murmured as he paused the movie. It was when they were about to find the first victim dead, bloody and mangled. The phone rang a third time. Logan picked up his new blue cordless halfway through the fourth ring.

"Hello?" Logan asked, only to silence. "Hello?" he asked again. He was about to hang up when he heard deep breathing, like having an asthma attack. Logan slammed down the phone angry with the prank, chipping the mouthpiece.

"Damn," he said, looking at the mouthpiece. "This was brand new." Logan went back to the living room and sat back down and restarted the first *Scream* movie. It had not even been on for five minutes when the phone rang again. Once again, Logan paused the movie and he walked to the kitchen and picked up the phone.

"Hello?" Logan was answered by the heavy breathing again. Logan was pissed that they were doing it again. "Hey, who the hell is this?" The breathing had stopped. "Listen you little faggot, you better not try this again or I'll star-69 your ass and come kick your little pussy ass!" The other end was silent.

Just as he was about to hang up the phone, a very muffled voice said, "You shouldn't call people bad names Logan it hurts their feelings, and threatening *me* with violence, now that's just plain stupid."

"H-How do you know my name?" Logan said, with fear in his voice.

"Oh, I know a lot of things about you, Logan." The voice said a little more clearly. "I know that tonight you are watching the *Scream* trilogy, and you are trying to lose weight for your wedding. I also know that you have three dogs,"

Logan was too scared for words.

"Two shiatsus and a lab Shepherd mix."

Logan finally swallowed his fear and spoke. "Whoever you are, I'm calling the police."

"Let's not jump to conclusions now, if you call the cops-and I will know-I will kill your Ann," said the man in a stern voice. The man chuckled as he heard Logan drop the phone.

Logan picked up the phone and in a trembling voice replied, "You don't have my fiancée."

"Really, I don't?" asked the man. "Ann is about 5'5, red hair, with blue eyes. That is your Ann right? If you need more convincing, listen to this."

"Logan! Help, he has a knife to my neck!"

a fearful woman screamed.

Logan was stunned into silence.

The man was back on the phone, "Now Logan, you will do everything I tell you or Ann will die. After that, I am coming for you, understand?"

Logan once again swallowed his fear. "Ok."

"Very good Logan, are you ready?" asked the man in a mocking voice.

Logan sighed. "Yes, what do I have to do?"

"First, I want you to cut all your phone lines, I will call you back on your cell phone," the man told him.

The phone then went dead.

Logan went to his garage and got some wire cutters, they had red rubber grips. Tears were beginning to run down his cheek. Then he went back inside and cut the phone line on his new wireless and his bedroom phone line. He put the cutters in his back pocket, picked up his cell phone and walked back downstairs. He sat back down in his Lay-Z boy recliner, and started to chug his beer while he waited. He turned off the TV; he was no longer in the mood for *Scream*.

After a minute or two he heard a phone ringing in the distance. Logan listened very closely and concluded that it was coming from the basement. He ran down and found out that he had forgotten to cut one of the phones. Logan reached out to answer it, his hand was shaking violently.

"Hello?" asked Logan

"Logan! You did not listen, I told you to cut all the phones and you just answered one, now Ann dies!"

"No, please give me another chance, you have to."

The man started laughing "You are pathetic, Logan, it makes me sick. Ok, because

I like you I will be nice and give you another chance," the man told him

"Thank you," Logan said happily. Thank you so much."

"Stop, stop I told you that makes me sick," said the man.

The phone then went dead. Logan hung it up, took the cutters out of his pocket, and cut the wire.

No sooner had he cut his phone than he heard the familiar ring of his cell phone. It was 'Jingle Bells', Ann's favorite song. Logan ran upstairs and answered it.

"Very good Logan, now I want you to lock all your windows and doors," the man told him.

"No way," Logan replied sternly.

"Yes, you will or Ann will die," said the man.

Logan was stunned into silence, but he did as the man told.

"I want you to hold the phone up so I can hear you lock all the doors, and windows. I will know if you don't lock one, you have ten combined locks," said the man.

Logan walked around the house and locked all the doors. A steady stream of tears was running down his cheeks. Logan knew what was going to happen to him; he just hoped that he could help Ann escape the same fate.

Click-one...Click-five...Click-ten.

"Very good, now I want you to go the attic and look in the big chest. You know the one that your dad gave you, the chest that your grandpa hand carved from oak."

The lighting flashed again, and less then an second later the thunder came; the storm was very close.

Logan walked up to the top floor, and went to the end of the hall. He reached up and pulled the cord hanging down. The stairs fell

down so fast they almost hit Logan in the head.
He walked up to the pitch black attic. Logan
felt around for the light switch. Once he found
it, he turned it on and light flooded into the
room. Logan spotted the chest in the back of
the attic. He walked to it and tried to open
it, but it wouldn't budge. Logan heard his cell
ringing. He ran down to get it, it was the man.

"Logan, you know you keep the chest
locked. Now go to you room and get the key out
of your old Nike shoebox. You know the one, in
the back of your closet," the man said, in an
almost pleasant voice, like the kind you use
when a little kid does something wrong.

Logan went to his room, got the key, and
ran back to the attic. When he got there he
realized he still had his cell phone in his
hand. He stared at it, thinking about what he
should do with it.

"You better open the chest soon," the man
said. For some reason the voice sounded closer,
like the man was in the attic with him.

The phone went dead; Logan put it in his
pocket. He walked back over to the chest, put
in the key, and turned it. He knew even before
he opened the lid, but he couldn't stop
himself. He looked inside and screamed.

Inside the chest was Ann's head. Her mouth
was twisted in a scream. The blood was dry-Ann
had been dead the entire time.

Logan was greeted by the hideous laugh of
the man.

"You bastard," Logan told the man.

"Now Logan," the man said. "I want you to
turn around for one more surprise."

Unable to think in his hysterical state,
Logan listened to the man, forgetting that he
had already hung up his cell phone. As soon as
Logan turned around he a saw knife coming
straight at his head. The knife went right

through his neck. Logan gurgled and fell forward landing beside the chest.

When his body hit the ground, a shadowy figure walked out from a corner. He had on a cowboy hat, trench coat and gloves, all of which were black leather. He stopped by Logan's lifeless body, and dropped a card into the puddle of blood gathering

Then he left the musty attic, which already had the faint smell of death lingering.

2

Clarke County Police Department

No one knows for sure what gave it away that something was wrong with the new neighbors. It may have been that the neighbors kept hearing the dogs barking, and sometimes crying. Or it could have been that the driveway was covered in so many newspapers all the different color bags made it look like there had been a party there. Whatever it was, someone called the Clarke County Police department to come check it out.

The phones at the Clarke County Police Department had been ringing off the hook all day. There was everything from bank robberies to home invasions to ransoms. Even for the town of Las Vegas it was a busy day for crime. It was quarter past 3:00 on Saturday December 6, 2003 when the calls went down to one or two calls every five to ten minutes. By 3:30 the calls had stopped all together. Everyone who worked in the field except Chief Powell and the rookie, Max, had left.

The chief was a man of short stature, with gray hair, green eyes and had the beginning of a mustache coming in. He was near his fiftieth birthday and rounded out at three hundred and fifty seven pounds.

"Aaaaa," said Chief Powell as he did a big stretch.

"I 'an 'inally relax, no 'on 'ere to
bother me 'cept the Ruke. He probably reading
dat book of his 'gain. So he won't bother me,"
he said to himself.

"Aaaaa," he said, as he did another big
stretch. Then he lay back in his chair, pulled
his hat over his face and closed his eyes.

The Chief was startled by return of the
calls.

"Ruke?" said the chief without getting up.

"Ruke, 'Et da god'am phone," he yelled
into the halls leading to the offices.

The phone continued to ring.

"Stupid ood for nothing," said the chief
as he straightened his hat and reached for the
phone.

"Ello? Clarke County Po-lise department,
Chief Powell 'peaking," he said. "ya-uh-ha," he
said as he was listening to the call.

"hat! Two week worth of mail, not
answering the door? We be right 'ere," he told
the caller.

"Ruke, Ruke, Ruke?" Wher de hell 're ya?"
yelled Chief Powell.

The chief started walking down the halls
peeking in each one. He had forgotten where the
rookie's office was. He had only been here for
about two weeks. The station had about fifty or
so offices so the Chief possibly had some work
to do,

"Ruke?" yelled the chief again. "Stupid
ruke probly lost in his book 'gain,"

The chief continued looking in offices.
Right before he was about to give up and go
alone he saw out of the corner of his eye
someone in an office. Chief Powell looked in
and there was the rookie reading his book. He
was spinning his badge between his middle and
index finger.

Ruke!" he yelled.

The rookie dropped his badge under his desk. He was the polar opposite of Chief Powell. He was thirty-three and had the tall lean makeup of a basketball player. He had a faint beard starting to come in, not more than a five o'clock shadow.

"Yes Sir," he answered.

"I been calling 'ou for five minutes, why didn't 'ou answer?" the chief asked.

"S-Sorry Sir I did not know that you were talking to me. I couldn't understand your accent, you have a very deep one sir," he replied.

"Well 'ou need to open your ears moe often, ruke," the chief told him.

"Uh-sir, I do have a name, it's Max," he told the chief.

"I know yer nam, you 'ave to earn the 'ight to be 'alled by it," he told Max.

"And another thing, technically I am not a rookie, before this I was a CSI for ten years, and a supervisor for three. I was one of the best there ever was."

"Than 'hy 'ou not 'orking as a CSI no more?"

"The only reason I am here is because last month I got a new boss. He was a real dick, he fired me because he did not like the way I collected and analyzed data and he made up some crap story about a scandal. He said that I was tampering with evidence to make the outcome I wanted, and accepting bribes. As soon as that was published ten years of a respectable reputation collapsed like a deck of cards." Max told the chief.

"Tuff luk ruke." He said not caring much, "This your first year at Clarke County, so to me 'ou a ruke,"

"OK," Max said, giving in. "What's the problem?"

"We done got a case, missing person. Two week no 'on knows wher they 're," said the chief.

"Really-no one?" Max asked.

"No, ter naybers kno wher they ar, we just checkin' out de place." said the chief with deep sarcasm.

"Alright," Max said realizing how stupid he just sounded. Max got up and buttoned his shirt, "wow two weeks."

"Stupid ruke, no 'onder he no longer CSI," said the Chief under his breath "Fascinated with a two week missin person case."

"Ok Chief, let me get my artillery belt, and we can go." Max said, as he ran after the chief.

Max gabbed his black leather belt. It had his nine mm, note pad, two pepper sprays, handcuffs, and extra cartridges on it. Then he grabbed his hat off the rack and left. They were in the car about to pull out when the chief looked at Max, and his face boiled to a very dark red, and he screamed.

"RUKE!!"

"Y-Yes sir," said the rookie, with fear in his voice and in his face.

"'Ou forgot somthin 'ery 'portant," he told Max.

"What?" asked Max.

"Look at yourself," said the chief.

Max looked at himself up and down.

"I have everything, Chief," Max said to him.

The chief's face got even redder than it was and he screamed.

"BADGE!"

"S-Sorry," said Max.

Then Max got out of the car, ran back inside, down all the halls to his office. He grabbed his badge from under his desk, pinned it on, and ran back out.

"Sorry again sir, I am so used to having my badge on my belt," said Max with a little fear still in his voice.

"Just 'ont let it 'appen gain," the chief told him.

They got to Logan's house about three minutes later. When they got there they got out of the cruiser and walked up the sidewalk towards the house. Chief Powell knocked on the front door. Then waited about two minutes. Then he tried the knob but it wouldn't budge. Then Powell and Max walked around the whole house and tried every window and door, not one would open. They then walked back to the front. Chief Powell knocked again and heard dogs bark.

"'and back ruke," he said, as he took out his gun. "Ha-ha. I've always 'anted to do this," said the chief.

The Chief shot the door handle and the bullet bounced right off, and nearly hit him.

"Shit, it always 'orks in them movies."

"Well that's the movies," Max said as he leaned down and picked up the mat reveling a key. "it never ceases to amaze me how many people hide their key in the most obvious place." He unlocked the door and they walked in. "Clarke County police anyone home?" he asked, there was no answer.

Then they saw two dogs run forward, they looked close to death. A black lab mix and a multicolored shiatsu. Max and Chief Powell looked through all the rooms and found nothing. On the way up to the attic they saw a third dog, also a shiatsu, it was light brown, and dead-long dead there were already holes in it where the bugs had started to eat the dead flesh.

While they were rechecking the top floor Max saw some plaster dust on the floor; he

pointed it out to the chief. They both looked
up and saw a dangling cord. The chief pulled it
an the stairs leading to the attic came
crashing down. The smell hit them like a wave.

    "Oh-Oh-Oh," they both said in unison.

    The smell was awful; they took a big
breath and walked up. At the top they
discovered the source of the smell.

    "'oly shit," said the chief as he heard
Max climb back down, run to the bathroom, and
vomit. "'hat 'de hell 're we dealing wit,"

3

An Old Grudge

"Sorry sir, I did not expect to see this." Max said.

"No worrie ruke….uhhhh, I tank I am going to vomit, t-take notes," the chief told him as he ran down to the bathroom and threw-up.

"Yes sir," Max told him as he took out his new note pad, flipped open the black leather cover and started.

•Male Caucasian, about 24, 25, can't tell natural hair color, dyed blonde. Cause of death rupture of the adrenal artery from knife wound. Look of blood and bloating of body been dead about two weeks-same as missing time.

Max wrote down then continued on to look in the chest the man was lying next to and gasped. In there was a head, he looked it over and wrote.

•Female Caucasian, red hair, green eyes. Cause of death most likely head cut off. Might be the same knife that killed the male. Too little evidence to tell how long she has been dead, probably two weeks like the male. Relation? Siblings? Boyfriend, girlfriend? Married? Engaged?

Max looked around and took a few more notes.

•Floor clean means that the female was not murdered here. Or the killer did a little cleaning before leaving the bodies.

Max then put away his notes and walked

down to where the chief was. He was sitting on
the toilet wiping his mouth. His face was still
pale and he looked like he was going to puke
again.

"I took notes on the victims sir," Max
told him.

"V-Victems? 'ere 'as moe then 'on?" Chief
Powell asked him.

"Yes sir, female head in the chest the
male was lying by."

"H-H-Her H-head vein 'anging oot….uhhhh,"
said the chief as he turned back around, opened
the toilet and puked again.

"All back up ruke," the chief said, as he
reached for a cup. Max hit his hand before he
could get one.

The chief was pissed, that Max had done
that to him.

"Ruke, 'hat de hell is wrong wit ye, let
me 'et a cup to 'et de tast out of me mouth,"
the chief said almost begging, and yelling at
the same time.

"Sorry Sir, we can't touch anything, it
could contaminate the crime scene. There is a
7-11 or something down the street, I think.
After I call for back up and CSI, I will run
down there and get you a water bottle, soda
sports drink, coffee, whatever you want Chief,
my treat," Max told him.

"How bout a bud?" asked Chief Powell.

"Not on duty, but I will pick up a six
pack for after." Max told him

"'ater han," said the chief.

"Ok, I will be right back." Max said

"Thak 'ou Max, dat would be great," the
chief replied.

"D-Did you just call me by my name,
Chief?" Max asked.

"Ya, 'ou erned it today, let see if ou can
eep it up. If ou eep it up, ou won't be called

ruke no more," the chief told him.

"Thank you sir, I won't let you down." Max said. "Like I care you stupid jackass." He said when he was out of earshot.

Max went down to the cruiser to call back up and for CSI to come.

"We have a code three, repeat we have a code three, a one eighty seven at 353 Windfrod Drive; Clarke County. I need back-up, a CSI, and a coroner," Max said into the speaker.

"Confirming address Alpha 2. That's 353 Windfrod drive?"

"Affirmative," Max said.

"Units will be there momentarily."

Max reholstered the speaker, then he drove up to the street and saw a Shell, Exxon, a BP, and a 7-11 at the end of the street he was now on.

Since the 7-11 was the closest he pulled up and topped off the tank before going in. He went right to the back where the cold drinks were and picked up two Deer Park spring waters and a six-pack of Bud. He went to the front to pay for them; then he drove back with the Bud on the floor. The chief was waiting outside the house. Max gave him a bottle. They both used about half the bottle to get the taste out and chugged the rest.

As soon as the CSIs got there, they got the yellow CRIME SCENE tape out and circled the whole house. Chief Powell and Max watched as they went inside and got to work. Chief Powell saw the last person walk in and he saw Max's facial expression turn to pure hate.

"Ou ok Max?" the Chief asked him.

"It's him, the bastard who fired me, my old supervisor." Max said.

Before the chief could stop him, Max ran up and stopped his old boss.

The man turned around, "What the…oh Max

it's you, ha-ha, you're a county cop now?" The
man was mostly bald with wrinkles beginning to
form; his glasses magnified his blue eyes. His
build was typical of someone his age.

"Yeah-yeah, laugh it up David, Vegas is in
Clarke County."

"Still a local," David interrupted.

"Getting rid of me was the worst mistake
of your life. I was one of the best in the
nation; you were just a dick who never liked
me. Too bad, you will need someone like me for
this case." Max told him.

"Yeah, how do you know that?" David asked.

"I have seen the newspapers, you have had
stuff way easier than this, and you didn't
solve them."

"I bet we can," said David, with a little
embarrassment in his voice.

"No, I don't think you can took notes, and
I saw nothing." Max said. "And you know how
good I am," he continued

"Sure Max, Sure," David said, as he walked
in.

"Hey David, there was something else I
wanted to tell you, what was it?" Max said,
rubbing his chin. "Oh-yeah, another thing the
newspapers said was that after I left, your
unsolved cases have gone up 5%,"

"So why should I be intimidated by you,
you're a stupid local now," David told him.

Max just looked at David for a while, then
charged him. Lucky for both of them, Chief
Powell stepped in front of Max and held him
back.

"'et in de car ruke, now!" the chief told
him. "ou suspended for two week, no pay." he
continued.

"But sir." Max said.

"No buts ruke, now get in the car," the
chief told him.

Max looked out the window and saw that David was looking at him, laughing.

"Screw you David," Max said.

Then Max threw his notes at David. They hit him in the back of the head.

"Ha-ha-ha, what now?" Max told David.

"RUKE!" Chief Powell yelled.

"Sir," Max replied.

"After 'hat little stunt, three week, still no pay."

"But…"

"All ready 'old ou, no buts," the chief said, before Max could finish.

"But Sir…"

"Don't sir me Ruke, less ou haunt four week."

Max said nothing, he just had that look on his face, that 'I will kill you' look.

The chief thought he saw it, but when he looked again Max had his regular face on. The Chief just thought it was a fluke, like when dogs do it sometimes.

When they got back to the station Chief Powell sat down at his desk while Max went down to his office. When the rookie came back out he walked up to the chief and said.

"Chief, please don't suspend me, I need the money, I have a family to support. Give me another chance."

"I will soon as 'ou come back, ruke." Chief Powell told him.

That look came back on his face and he said, "Well you know what, I don't need this shit, I can find another job. See you in hell you stupid redneck."

Then the chief saw Max walk back toward his office. He heard his locker open and slam shut. Max came back a few minutes later with his box of stuff.

"I left that stupid uniform in my locker.

You can pick it up for your next "Ruke", Max said.

"How dar ou make fun of me," said the chief.

Max did not hear him; he was already out the door.

Then he walked back in and threw something at Chief Powell and said.

"I almost forgot to give you back this stupid badge," He said.

Then he left.

Chief Powell watched him as he pulled out, and swore he saw Max giving him the finger.

4

The Crime Scene

When Max got home he threw the box that had all his police stuff on his desk in his den and then he walked up to his room. His wife and kids would still be up, it was Saturday. They always watched SNL, it was one of their favorite shows. When he opened the door there they were, his wife Sue was in bed and his two kids, Dan and Bill, were laying on the floor. Sue was the same age as Max. She has red shoulder length hair, her blue eyes gleamed like the sea. Dan looked like a mini Max. Right down to those green eyes. Bill, on the other hand, had Max's hair but his mom's eyes. And kind of a mix of Max and Sue for his nose and smile.

"Dad!" Dan and Bill said as they ran up to him.

"Hey guys, how you been doing?" Max asked.

"Good," they said in unison.

"Hey sweetie," Max said to Sue, then kissed her.

"I have to talk to you," he whispered in her ear.

"Boys, could you watch the end of SNL in your room, your dad and I need to talk." Sue said.

Dan and Bill did not say anything, they just kissed their parents goodnight and went to their rooms.

"Yes?" said Sue.

"I-I quit my job today, I don't know what we are going to do." said Max.

"You quit?" asked Sue.

"Yes, Chief Powell was going to suspend me for three weeks, without pay." said Max.

"Why?" asked Sue

"I almost got in a fight with my old boss, David, at a crime scene, then threw the notes I took at him." he said.

"Oh, I don't know, maybe if we wait someone might take you, you were a great CSI," said Sue.

"Yeah, you are right I suppose," said Max.

Max climbed into bed and before Sue had a chance to turn off the light he was fast asleep.

The next day when Max came back from the store Sue was smiling.

"What is it?" Max asked her putting down the bags of groceries.

"Check your messages, I think you will be pleased," said Sue.

Max walked over to his answering machine and pressed play.

"Uh yeah Max, this is David, I think you were right we might need you for this case. If you come back, I will give you a raise and will let you collect and analyze the evidence any way you want. Call me back when you get the chance,"

Max picked up his phone and called David, after three rings he picked up.

"Hello, David Walker," he said.

"Yeah David, it's Max, I was calling for the job," he said.

"Max, so glad to hear you want to come back, when can you start?" David asked.

"Whenever you want, I owe you one for letting me come back," said Max.

"Ok, how about the crime scene in about three hours?" asked David.

"Ok I will see you there," said Max.

Max then hung up the phone.

"Got my job back," he said to Sue laughing.

When Max got to the crime scene hours David was already there.

"Hey Max, I brought your badge and tools," said David.

"I still can not thank you enough for giving me my job back," said Max

"No problem, I really do need you for this one, there is nothing that we can see," David said.

"Wait, before we get started we have to set a few things straight."

"Ok, what do you want?"

"You killed my reputation. You said I was manipulating evidence and taking bribes. Why did you do it?"

David turned red, "About that I-I um recently found out that my source was a bad one, and that there was never any backing to that claim."

"So when were you going to tell the press this?" Max inquired impatiently.

"I had a scheduled press conference in three weeks, just after I got back from my brothers wedding."

"And then what?"

"Well, this happened and I decided to move it up to tomorrow."

"Really?" Max said with hope.

"Yes, tomorrow I am going to admit my mistake.

"Do I get my job back as supervisor of the swing shift?"

"No I am sorry but that position has already been filled, but I can guarantee you an office and promise that when a supervisor shift becomes available you will be the first to know."

Max smiled and shook David's hand, "Ok, let's get started."

They then walked up to the yellow CRIME SCENE DO NOT CROSS tape and went in.

"First things first, what have you done yet, and what rooms haven't you done?" asked Max.

"We only did the attic, and we just scanned the area around the body," David told him.

"We also already bagged the knife, we got a good solid print on it," he continued.

"Good, let's go check it out," said Max.

Max started looking around on the way up to the attic to make sure there wasn't anything there. All he saw were boxes along the wall that had yet to be unpacked. "Damn, they never even got a chance to finish unpacking," Max stopped. "this means that the killer knew them."

David jotted that down, "Good call my men missed that."

"So how did the killer get in anyway?" asked Max.

"Don't know, all the doors are locked and there is no sign of forced entry," said David.

When they got to the attic they put on their gloves and got started.

They got their flashlights and walked slowly over the floor, looking for some sort of trace. David saw Max stop and bend down and started looking at something.

"Got something?" asked David.

"Yes, I think it is some kind of fabric or something stuck on a nail." said Max. He turned around, opened his metal tool case, and took out a magnifying glass and some tweezers. He then went back over to the spot he was looking at and held the magnifying glass over it.

"Yep, this is part of someone's clothes," said Max.

"What kind of fabric is it?" asked David. "It might help us know where to look for a suspect, by the kind or cost," he continued.

"I think it is just regular leather, but let's bag it and send it to the lab just in case," said Max. He put the leather in a plastic bag, then in his briefcase and went back to look for more traces.

"So how were you able to come back so easily, I know you have a different job now as a local?" asked David.

"Well, after I tried to beat you up, I got suspended for two weeks. Then I saw you laughing, and I thought it was at me so I threw my notes at you, which I am very sorry about, he gave me three weeks no pay. Then he wouldn't even let me explain. When we got back to the station I tried to get out of it again, but he wouldn't let me so I said, 'I don't have to take this shit. See you in hell you stupid redneck.' Then I got my stuff and left."

"Oh, and for the record, I was not laughing at you, I was laughing at a joke I heard, a very funny one," said David.

"Lets hear it," said Max.

David told him a mundane joke about a man and a bar, barley keeping his composer at the punch line.

Max did not find it humorous, but he gave a little laugh anyway, and they went back to gathering evidence. Twenty minutes later David stopped and saw something.

"Max, will you please get me a black light and a swab, I found a spot of something," said David.

Max did as he was told, and when David

shone the black light there was a slight glow, but nothing to tell if something was there.

"On second thought, could you get me some Luminol so we can see if there is any blood around?" asked David.

Max went over and picked up the bottle and tossed it to David. He sprayed it and a patch started to glow, David sprayed it a few more times and they both gasped. A gigantic blue cloud opened up on the floor. David sprayed a few more times and followed the trail. The blue trail went straight to a box in the corner. David went to the box, opened it and gasped.

"What is it?" asked Max.

"I think I found the female's body," said David wincing.

"What?!" said Max incredulously.

Max went over and saw it for himself. The body was green and brown, it was so bloated it looked like the simplest touch would make it explode.

"Could you go and call the coroner to come pick her up?" asked David.

"Sure," said Max.

Max ran down and called for the coroner, then went back up.

"I think we should stop for the day," said David.

Max did not want to but agreed.

"Can I drive the evidence back to the lab?" asked Max.

"Sure why not," said David.

As they left Max looked down and started to stare at the floor.

"What's that?" Max asked, pointing to a part of dried up blood that was slightly higher up than the rest.

"Don't know, must have skipped right over it." David said.

Max and David walked over to it and

kneeled down to take a closer look. He first took out the camera and took pictures from several different angles. Then he took out a x-acto knife and started to carefully cut around the shape. Then he got some tweezers and slowly put them under it, and lifted it up. It was had a little blood on it, but Max could still make it out; it was a playing card-An ace of spades.

"Do you know what this means?" asked Max.

"No," answered David.

"The ace of spades is the death card, and this is probably our killers calling card," Max said.

"You mean that this could be a serial?"

"God let us pray against that." Max replied.

After Max bagged it and put it away they left. On the way down Max was still looking around the walls and doors. When they got outside they put it in Max's truck and left after the coroner did.

Just before David got home, he got a call on his radio. "We have a 10-53, repeat we have a 10-53 at the corner of 5th and Grand. We need an ambulance, and backup stat."

10-53? That's an officer down. David pulled a U-turn and went speeding the other way, trying not to think about who it might be. When he got there he got out and stepped on something. He looked down; it was a badge with an ID attached. He gasped when he read the number-683-he had no need to look at the picture. He knew whose badge it was, he had just seen it today.

It belonged to Max

5

The Hospital

David could not believe that he was holding Max's badge. He slowly walked over to the car and saw Max sitting beside it with a knife slightly to the left of his right shoulder.

"Max, are you ok?" asked David.

"Da-Da-David, help I need to go t-to a hospital," said Max gasping for breath.

"It's on the way, Max, you just need to hold on for a few more minutes," David said.

"Yes," said Max. "I also have to apologize, I grabbed the knife to try to pull it out."

"Its Ok don't apologize, who did this to you?" asked David as he got out his note pad.

"Didn't see his face, but after he stabbed me, he lit the evidence box on fire its on the side of the road," said Max.

David quickly took the notes as he put the notes away Max fell over. David rushed over and was relived to feel a pulse. Then he sat down beside the car and waited. When he propped Max back up, so he would not lose any more blood, he noticed something; there was a playing card in front of the handle of the knife. He looked closely at it, there was one little corner without blood; it was another ace of spades-they had a serial killer on their hands. When the ambulance got there, David helped load in Max, then went to his house. When he got there, he noticed that all of the lights were off-no one had called his wife. David walked up to the door and rang the bell. In a few minutes Max's wife answered the door.

"Yes?" she asked sleepily.

"Mrs. Levinton?" asked David.

"Yes, what do you need?" she said.

"My name is David Walker, I have some news about Max," he said slowly.

"Max!" she was now fully awake.

"Yes Ma'am, I got a call for a man down, and it was your husband," he told her.

"Is he dead?" Sue asked with fear and worry in her voice.

"No, but he lost a lot of blood; he was stabbed in the shoulder." David said.

"Well, where is he?" Sue asked.

"He is in Clarke County hospital. If you want I can drive you up right now." David said.

"Thank you, that would be great, let me get a coat," answered Sue.

When they were on their way there Sue wanted to know more about Max.

"Well, he lost a whole lot of blood and…"

"Yeah I know that already, how do you know him?" Sue asked.

"Oh, sorry I am his boss," David said.

"Oh, do we know who stabbed him?" Sue asked.

"We think it was the person who killed the people at the crime scene that he found and investigated today." David answered.

"How is that possible?" Sue asked.

"Well we don't know, but he told me that he was stabbed, and then the guy lit the evidence box on fire," David told her.

"How did the killer get to him?" Sue asked.

"I don't know, I was going to ask him that but he passed out," said David.

"Well we are here," David announced as they pulled into the parking lot.

"Thank you, David," Sue said

"You're welcome," he said.

Sue was walking in and realized that David was walking in behind her.

"I don't need any more help, David," Sue said.

"I know, I am staying to see my #1 investigator, I want to make sure he is ok," David told her.

When they got in they went to the desk.

"Max Levinton please," Sue said.

"Mr. Levinton is in room 317 on the third floor," said the receptionist.

"Thank you."

They were on the way to the elevator when they heard the PA come on and say.

"Code blue, we have a code blue in room 317, stabbing victim; we need all emergency personal immediately." Then the PA went off.

David and Sue looked at each other and both said,

"Oh my God."

They forgot about the elevator and ran up the stairs. When they got to the third floor they saw them wheeling Max out. They ran with them.

"Let me in, he is my husband," Sue said.

"Ok, you can come but the other man has to wait," the doctor said.

"Wait he…" Sue tried to say.

"It's alright, Mrs. Levinton, he is more important to you," David said.

"Ok, thank you again for everything you have done today," said Sue.

"Don't mention it, it was no problem," David told her.

Then he saw them disappear into the operating room. They had only been together for

a half hour, but it had seemed that they had
been friends forever.

The ER was in a frenzy trying to bring Max
back to life. Sue was not actually in the room,
she was watching through a little window. She
almost left because all the blood was making
her sick, but the thing that made her stay was
her love for her husband. They had clogged up
the blood, and had sewn him back up, but Max
was still a flat liner.

"Clear!" yelled one of the doctors as they
rubbed the defibrillator together. Max's body
jumped up as the defibrillator shocked his
body.

"Still no pulse," yelled the doctor.

"Clear!" the doctor yelled again-Max's
body was shocked once more.

The monitor started beeping as Max's pulse
came back.

"We got a pulse," one of the doctors said.

"Take him to ICU, and keep an eye on his
monitors," one of the other doctors ordered.

"Ok, which room will he be in?" Sue asked
as they wheeled him out.

"You can just follow us," the doctor
replied.

They then hooked all the life support
machines to carts and started to wheel Max out
of the ER. When they had passed about two halls
of doors they stopped and wheeled him into room
317 in the ICU. When were all in they put Max
on the bed and left. Sue sat down behind her
husband, and held his hand. Within a few
minutes she heard the door open. Sue looked
over and saw a nurse walk in.

"Hi, Mrs. Levinton, is it?" asked the
nurse.

"Yes, who are you?" she replied.

"My name is Holly, nice to meet you," she
held her hand out to Sue, they shook and Holly

took a seat by the edge of the bed.

"If you don't mind telling me, how did this happen?" Holly asked.

"I really don't know." Sue answered. "I was at home when his boss came and told me what had happened. He said that it was probably the same man who killed the victims at the crime scene he investigated today.

"Wow who was murdered?" Holly asked.

"I don't know, he never tells me, and he was stabbed before he got home," Sue said. "I don't think they have identified the bodies yet. When they do they will first notify the families. Then they might put it on the news" Sue continued.

"Huh." said Holly.

Then Holly got out a book and started to read. Sue was going to go to sleep when her cell started to ring.

"Hello?"

"Mrs. Levinton, it's Ben I didn't see any cars leave this morning, is everything OK?"

Shit Susan thought, she had forgotten about the kids. "Ben I am at the hospital, Max got hurt last night."

"Is he OK?"

"Yeah he is just fine, could you or Carol do me a favor and get the kids ready for school?"

"No problem," Ben replied.

"Thanks Ben."

"Don't mention it, I will see you tonight."

"OK, bye Ben."

"Bye Sue."

Sue then hung up the phone, then she leaned back and went to sleep. When she woke up Max was awake and eating breakfast. When he noticed Sue he looked over and smiled.

"Hi honey," he said.

"Hi."

"When did you get here?" he asked.

"Around twelve maybe," she said.

"Oh."

"You might not remember, but last night for a few minutes you flat lined."

"I was dead?"

At that moment David walked in.

"How are you doing Max? We had a scare last night."

"Yes I am fine now, thank you."

"Now I hate to do this but I must take notes while the memory is still fresh," David said.

"Ok. I was driving to the lab when I noticed that there was a car on the side of the road. I could not just leave him there so I pulled over to see if I could help. He told that his transmission was shot and it would be nice if he could get a ride to the nearest gas station. When he got in he dropped something on the floor. He reached down to grab it, and I don't know how to put this, have you read the *Dark Tower* books?"

When David nodded his head Max went on, "It was like he was a real Roland; his speed with that knife was incredible-I could not even see him. But I felt a sharp sting and looked over and saw the knife right by my shoulder. Then he pushed me out and got the keys. I watched as he went to the back of the truck. After a little while he came back and took my badge. Then he got in his car and left. After what seemed like an eternity I could smell something burning and it clicked-he had destroyed the evidence. The strange thing is that I could not see his face. He had on a overcoat that looked kind of like the fabric we found. He also had on a big hat that covered his face."

"Is that all?" asked David.

"Oh yeah, I think he had some kind of small sized car. It could have been blue of black but it was too dark to tell."

"That does not help much but it will when we get a suspect," David said. "Thank you Max, these notes will help the instigation, now you can take as much time as you need off to let your wound heal. Then I need you back, you helped us get stuff we did not find with five other guys working the same scene." David told him

"Ok, thank you. I think I should be back within a few weeks."

"No, I don't want you pushing it, take as long as you want off."

"Wow, you really are a great boss," Max said.

"Thanks that means a lot to me," David said, walking out. David went down the stairs and into the parking lot and walked to his car, a red corvette, got in and started to drive towards the lab. David had never had a case like this (when an investigator was attacked by the suspect) and in the pit of his stomach he was a little nervous about working this case.

6

The Autopsies

When David was halfway to the crime lab his pager started to go off. David picked it up and pressed the button to turn it on. The little screen glowed green and Larry's, the coroner, number came up. David picked up his phone, and scrolled down until he found Larry's number. After two rings Larry picked up.

"Hello? Larry Small."

"Larry, this is David, what do you need?"

"Yes, David, could you come over here soon I would like to start the autopsies. I already searched for trace and came up with a goose egg."

"Nothing?"

"Not a thing-you've got a tough one here."

David sighed, "Alright, maybe we'll have better luck with the autopsies."

"I'm pulling for you-see you in a few minutes."

"I'll see you."

David closed his phone and continued towards the lab. When he got there he had no trouble finding a spot; he had hit it at the time where the night shift is over but the day had yet to begin, so there were not many cars. One of the cars he recognized was an eighty-two blue Mustang, it belonged to Larry. That was what David liked about him; he always came early and worked late even though he wasn't asked to. David thought it helped Larry keep his mind off his wife.

 She had died about four years ago; in a
drunk driving accident. Larry was devastated,
he really loved her, and so did everyone else.
David was not here then, but he heard that he
cried non stop for months. She was supposed to
be one of the nicest people who ever lived.
When he finally came back, he started working
his ass off not asking for any extra money.
Even when Gerald, the old head, offered it he
refused. David guessed he did it because he did
not want any one else to feel the same pain he
did. The pain that gets you right in the
stomach that makes you want to puke thinking
that there is other people out there like the
one that killed your loved one. So he tried to
help out with all the cases he could. Max was
the one who finally found the guy. He traced
the tire tracks and the paint transfer on the
passenger side of Larry's car to an AA sponsor
of all people. The man took a deal for one year
in jail and eighteen months probation for
negligence and vehicular manslaughter.

 When David went in, he went into his
office put his stuff down, and brought out
Max's file to fix it when the autopsies were
over. When he got to the morgue he put on latex
gloves, a white lab coat and went in. He saw
Larry just finishing washing down the male
body; the female was laying on the table beside
him. He watched Larry finish washing down the
body-David had always found it weird how they
washed down the body. They used a shower head
with a rope on it, like the ones you find in
the handicap showers. The body was so bloated
that David could not tell which part of the
face he was looking at.

 After Larry was done he went to move the
body to the steel table. Larry had brown hair
that was gray at the roots; his age had made a

horseshoe out of his hair.

"David, I am ready to start if you are," Larry said.

"Lets start," David replied.

"Ok, let's start with the big Y."

David watched as Larry made one slit from each shoulder meeting at the chest, then one straight down to the pelvis. When he flipped the skin back it was even more disgusting, the inside of the skin was green and it looked like the veins were pushed up against the skin, and the smell!

David did not know how Larry could stand it. He felt like puking, but it seemed that Larry did not smell it. Maybe it was because he had been doing it for the past thirty years or so, David didn't know. David watched as Larry sawed straight through the ribs, like he had with the skin, but not as easy. Then Larry moved the two halves of ribs to the sides like he did with the skin, he got out some clamps and clamped the skin and ribs so they would not fall back in place during the autopsy.

"Ok, let's start with a blood and tissue sample, then on to the organs, finishing with the brain."

Larry took a small blood and tissue sample, tagged it and put it beside David. Then he started to take out the organs one by one, checking them and weighing them. When Larry had finished checking all the organs, he put them back in place. Then he carefully put the ribs back in place. After that, he folded the skin back and sewed it back.

"Ok, now let's check the head," Larry said, as they carefully turned over the body. Larry got back out the knife and started to cut the skin off the back of the skull and flipped the skin back. Then he went to get the high speed oscillating saw and started to cut the skull open. David turned around for the next part as he had always hated it. He heard Larry walk over and pick something up off the table, then walk back over to the body. He slipped the chisel under the skull and pulled; the skull popped right off exposing the brain. When he was sure it was over he turned back around, Larry was already holding the grayish-green brain. He weighed it like the rest of the organs then put it back.

"Look here," he said pointing to the neck where the knife went in. "The knife entered in though the front at a near one hundred and eighty degree angle. Upon entry the carotid artery was severed resluting in near immedate death."

"Are we going to do the female now?" David asked.

"Yes, but first I need to make an impression of the teeth," Larry said.

Then he took out a mouth guard like object and pushed it against the top and bottom teeth. He bagged and tagged the impression, then he zipped back up the body bag and pushed it back into the freezer. David moved over to the table where there were two separate bags.

"Why are there two bags?" David asked.

"One is the body, the other one is the head." Larry replied.

"Why didn't you sew the head back on the body yet?"

"I will, but first I like to look at the body the way it was left to us," Larry said.

David helped Larry move the female body bag to the steel table so he could wash it. Then he unzipped the bag and put the body on the table, and started to wash it down. The female was so bloated that David was surprised that it didn't explode. When he finished with the body, he got out the head and washed it down as well. When Larry started to do the 'big Y' there was a little hiss and some gasses came out. Then he did all the same things he did with the male, he took a blood and tissue sample, took out the organs weighed them and put them back. Then he sewed the body back up and started to put it back in the bag. While he was zipping it up the arm fell out.

"Whoops," Larry said, as he leaned over to put it back in the bag.

"Wait, what is this?" he said, looking at the nails.

"My God," Larry continued.

"What?"

"Look over here, do you see the blue skin under the nails?" Larry asked.

"Whoa, doesn't that mean that she was suffocated?"

"Yes only..." Larry went over to the table and got the head.

"Yep, the lips are blue too.

"I just don't get why I didn't see this at the scene or when I was washing it," Larry continued.

"So if she died of suffocation, why was the head cut off?"

"Our killer did it to throw us off track." Larry said. "It also means that our killer is an amateur, he thought with cutting off the head, it would throw us off track."

Then he made dental impressions with the female and bagged them both.

"Will you run these over to trace for me?"

"Sure," David said, getting the bag.

"Oh and tell Max I hope he is back soon, haven't seen that kid for a few months," said Larry. "Didn't he get his start from the Orange Creek killings?"

"Yes he was only a rookie and found what most veterans did not, that is why he has been regarded as one of the best since he started."

Then David left, and dropped the imprints off at Eddie's lab. He was young like Max, with red hair, brown eyes and glasses. He had a fairly nice lab with all the modern tools. He had AFIS (Automated Fingerprint Identification system), CODIS (Combined DNA Index System) a small glue fume (Super glue is heated and it fumes up into an enclosed box and prints appear on what they have, if any), and IBIS (Integrated Ballistics Identification System) to compare bullets. He also had some of the basics like microscopes.

Three weeks later while David was eating lunch at one of the local dinners his pager beeped. He picked it up and saw Larry's number. His picked up his phone and called him.

"Hello?"

"Hi Larry, did you page me?"

"Yes, I got the toxic screen back on the victim; he was mildly intoxicated at the time of death."

"Thanks, anything will help."

As soon as David hung up his phone, his beeper started to go off again. He looked at the number; it was Eddie's. David scrolled down and dialed him too.

"Hello?"

"Hi Eddie; its David."

"David, just paged you."

"Well?" he said, taking a sip of coke.

"I got the identification for your vics. Sorry it took so long, I was backed up, and I took a while to find a match."

"Well?" David asked.

"Are you sitting down?"

David did not like where this was going, "Yes, but why?"

"I um…don't know how to tell you this, but the male is Logan, your brother, the female is

Ann, your future sister-in-law," Eddie said.

As soon as David heard those names he dropped his cell and the drink he had in his other hand. The cup dropped to the ground and shattered and sent glass and coke everywhere. David could still hear Eddie as his phone dropped to the ground.

"David-Dav..." No more came out the cell phone collided with the ground shattering the face and drowning the chip.

7

The Plan

"Sir, Sir are you ok?" asked someone touching his shoulder with tenderness like you would touch a baby. David turned around to see an employee with a mop and another with a broom and dust pan.

"What? Huh-huh y-yes I am-am fine," David said, on the verge on tears, he was using all of his strength to keep from crying. The lasting image of his brother would be his body on that autopsy table.

"Are you sure? You dropped your cup on the floor, and then dropped your phone into it. It must have been bad news, it looked like a pretty expensive phone," she said.

"No, everything is fine," he said. *Except I just found out my brother was murdered*, he thought as he picked up his cell phone. He picked it up out of the puddle and slipped it in his pocket-he still had some time on his warranty-he would get a new one in the morning.

It was then when David noticed that she had a mop and dustpan. "I can get that, after all I spilled the coke," David said.

"No, sir don't worry about it," she swept up the soda and the man swept up the glass as David walked out, "have a nice day," they called but David was too far gone.

When David got into his car he could not hold it back anymore, he put his head on the steering wheel and bawled.

After a few minutes, David lifted his head and was able to hold back his tears. He buckled up and left the parking lot, then he drove around for a little bit. After a few minutes he saw what he was looking for, a phone booth. There was nowhere to pull over on the side of the road, so he drove to the closest parking lot. It was about twenty yards away. Before he got out he made sure he had enough money. He shook his pocket a little and heard the muffled sound of coins. Then he got out and made his way towards the phone booth. This news would hit his mom really hard; two years ago his dad had died of a pulmonary embolism. His mom had been visiting her sister, and no one was there when he left. When he got there he took a deep breath, let it out with a sigh and walked in. He put in the first two quarters and dialed his mom's number. His mom lived across the country in North Carolina. After three rings he heard the click of someone picking up the phone.

"Hello?" answered a female voice.

"Mom?"

"Yes, is this David or Logan?"

"It is David, Mom, I have some news that you might not take so well."

"What, did your brother and that Ann girl break up while in the Bahamas?"

David's mom always had referred to Ann as "that Ann girl" ever since Logan had first brought her home. David did not know why, but his mom had always hated Ann. It made no sense as she was the nicest girl, and Logan was crazy about her, but his mom had made no attempt to try to like her. She probably thought of David's old girlfriend, who had left him in the middle of the night four months into their relationship. She also got away with his bank card and three thousand dollars of his money.

"That's the thing, Mom, they never went."

"What do you mean?" she asked. "We were supposed to go up there next week for their wedding."

"Mom, Logan and Ann are dead, they were uh...murdered."

"NO! IT'S NOT TRUE, IT CAN'T BE, MY BABY IS NOT DEAD, HE WAS SO YOUNG!" she screamed. "So young," she finished in a whisper.

"Mom? I need you to come down here, it might be hard, but we will get through it together just like with Dad. I will have to go; I need to talk to Ann's parents too."

"O-ok I will try to fly out to-to ni-hiiiight," she hung up the phone crying.

Then David walked back to his car and started to drive to Ann's house. When he got there he walked up to the front door and rang the bell.

A woman of about forty answered it.

"Yes, may I help you?"

"My name is David Walker, I am with the Las Vegas crime lab, I have some news for you. Is your husband here? You might want to be together for this."

"Yeah-yeah sure, Allen!"

A man walked up.

"I don't know how to tell you this, but your daughter along with my brother was murdered before they went to the Bahamas," David said.

Ann's mom collapsed into her husbands arms.

"No she is not dead. SHE CANNOT BE DEAD!" screamed her dad.

Then they closed the door, David heard Ann's dad carry her mom back to the living room.

As David walked back to his car he still could not believe that he was working a case with his brother as the victim! And the other

as his future sister-in-law! In all his years
as a criminologist, he never thought he would
have to make that horrible phone call about
someone he knew. You just don't think about
those kinds of things.

David did not know what he was going to
do; he was emotionally involved with this case.
David really wanted to work this for this
family and he wanted to find that son of a
bitch that killed his brother and future
sister-in-law, and make him or them pay. Also
he wanted to keep as many people as possible
from having to feel the same way he does,
because as of now this one had the makings of a
serial. So far, there had been two major
attacks both, with an ace of spades, one
leaving two people dead.

David was about halfway back to the crime
lab when he decided what he was going to do. No
one but Eddie knew that the victims were his
brother and future sister-in-law. So if he
never told anyone-they would never know.

There was only one problem though, how
would he get all the evidence analyzed? He was
pondering the solution when his beeper went
off. He checked the number it was Max. Max.
That was it. He could get Max to do it. Max
could go to Eddie's lab, and find out
everything then come back and tell him all he
needed to know. It was foolproof. David just
hoped that Max would recover soon.

As David walked into the crime lab, his
beeper went off. He jogged into his office and
dialed Max.

"Hello?"

"Hey Max, its David, you paged?

"Hey, Yes, I think that I might be able to
come back soon."

"Oh thank God," David said without
thinking.

"Whoa, miss me that much?"

"Yeah, yeah that's it," said David, hitting himself in the head for being so stupid, he almost ruined his plan.

"If it is all right, can I come back soon?" asked Max.

"Are you sure? I mean are you at 100%?" asked David.

"I'm sure I am fine, I was able to take the band-aids off a few days ago."

"Ok, if you really think you are fine, you can start as early as tomorrow," David told him.

"OK, will see you then. Bye."

"Bye Max."

David hung up the phone and walked around the crime lab, praying to God his plan would work, and he could still work this case.

8

Execution

When David walked in he was sure to sneak past Eddie, he knew the rules about knowing the victims. If you knew the victim you could not work the case. Lucky for him Eddie was not here right now, he let out a sigh of relief and walked into his office. Then he got out the case files and started to look them over. It just did not make sense; there were no clues at all-this guy was a pro. David looked over the notes and pictures he had taken for the next few hours and still nothing. David took out his glasses and rubbed his eyes, he was tired. He looked at his watch and found out why; it was almost 11:30, he had been looking over the files for eight hours, He must have zoned out. He put the files back in his file cabinet, then walked out of the room, and bumped right into Eddie.

"Whoa, easy there David, what's the hurry?" Eddie asked.

"Nothing, just trying to get home, I am pretty tired," David replied.

"Yeah, I am still trying to get used to being up at this time again, I work the swing shift now, getting off in thirty minutes."

"Yeah, I guess the shock of losing my brother got to me," David said.

"I am so sorry about that, man, is there anything I can do for you?" Eddie said, patting David on the back.

"No thanks, I will be fine."

"Ok, hey, why are you here anyway, you can't work this case anymore?"

"I *am* the head, and there are cases other then this one."

"Ok whatever," Eddie said, walking into his lab.

That was a close one David thought.

When he got home his mom was already there.

"Oh David," said his mom, before she broke out crying as she ran into his arms.

"It's ok, it's ok," he said, rubbing her back.

The next morning David snuck out as quietly as possible, his mom had been up half the night crying. She needed some sleep. When David was about to close the door he heard his home phone ring, he walked back in and picked it up.

"Hello, David Walker."

"Thank God you are OK. We did not know what to do, we couldn't reach you on your cell."

David heard Max put his hand over the receiver lightly because he could still hear.

"He's fine."

"Could you hurry up and get here, so we could go over the evidence with Eddie?"

"How long have you been there?"

"About an hour, just looking at the case file you put on my desk. God, it's good to be back," Max said.

"An hour! It's pretty early."

"No, actually it's about three."

"What!"

"Yeah, no one knew where you were; finally we decided to call to make sure everything was all right. Is it?" Max asked.

"Yes thank you. I just overslept; I didn't

know how late it was."

"Ok, if I am not there when you arrive, I am out getting lunch."

"You don't have to wait to go over the evidence; you can just tell me what he said."

"Ok, you sure?" asked Max.

"Yep go ahead I will be late; I have not left home yet."

"Alright, I will fill you in when you get here.

"Ok bye," said David.

"Bye."

David hung up the phone and walked out happier than he had been in a while. His over-sleeping helped him with the plan. He hoped he could think of more reasons to skip Eddie, for next time.

When David got to the lab he saw Max in his office, leaning back in his chair sipping on his drink. A burger paper was stuffed in the fry box. David knocked on the inside wall. Max jumped up spilling some soda on his shirt.

"Son of a…Oh hi David."

"Hi Max, so what do you have on the case so far?" asked David

"Pull up a chair and I'll fill you in."

David went into his office, got a chair and went back into Max's.

"Ok, first of all there nothing to find out because the evidence was burned."

"Oh, yeah," David said.

"However, our only lead is that ace of spades that was under the knife."

"That's all?" David asked.

"Well yes, we have no evidence," Max replied.

"Ok, I will see you later," David said, picking up the chair.

When David was halfway to the door he heard Max speak.

"By the way David, when were you planning on telling me that the victims were your brother Logan and his fiancée Ann?"

David stopped dead in his tracks, and his blood froze with fear.

Part Two:
Rob and Denise

All truth is not to be told at all times.
                              -Samuel Butler

9

A Sickness

The lights, the beeps and whistles, and the screaming winners-the sound of the casino; a sound that Rob had tried to hear way too often; Rob was addicted to gambling. He loved it all, the slots, blackjack, poker, and craps, anything that could get him more money. The only problem was that it never happened, the money he gambled, he always lost. It had started when he was twenty-one, it was spring vacation. He was dying to gamble from the first minute, but the problem was he had no extra money, all of it was going to his hotel, but one day he found a quarter on the floor.

A quarter, it had started as simple as that. After he found the quarter, he walked around for a bit until he found the quarter slots. He put it in and the lights went crazy; he won the twenty-five thousand dollar jackpot.

That was all it took-after that he could not get enough. He had it so bad that that summer after he had graduated from college, he moved to a small town outside of Vegas. The worst part was when he was at the casinos; he was hit with the double whammy. He also became addicted to alcohol. It started because that was all they served one a day two... five...nine he was up to around twenty a day. Most of his paycheck went to it and his account was almost empty. Rob was well on his way to becoming a bum. A bum that used all his change he got for gambling. That was Rob, the Rob before Denise.

Everything changed when they met. She had helped him beat it one step at a time. She cut his cash down big time. She limited him to fifty a week in the casino. After a few weeks, she cut it down to twenty, then ten and so on and so forth until she had him off gambling altogether. The alcohol was another story. She tried to help in the same way she helped with the gambling, but that did not work the same way. Like most alcoholics, he had bottles hidden all around the house. One day Denise had him empty all of them down the sink and then she sent him to rehab. While he was gone Denise turned the house upside down to make sure he had dumped them all, sure enough, she found a dozen more bottles of hard liquor. A few weeks after he came back, he proposed. They were married four months later. Yep things were really going their way.

Rob was in the living room watching wildcard weekend pre-game show. Terry was arguing with Howie about who was the best team or something like that. Rob did not always understand the rants they went on. The game was set to start in five minutes; Panthers vs. Cowboys. He was all set. He had all his snacks and his gear. He was a die-hard Panthers fan. He had been with them from the beginning. He had been there when they shocked America by making it to the NFC championship in their second year, (a NFL record) and he had stuck with them through their 1-15 season. Now after seven years, they were finally back in the playoffs.

Denise was upstairs watching some Lifetime movie. Rob did not know which one, but he felt bad. Why so, he did not know, but for some reason he felt like he should be with her. He turned off the pre-game show and walked

upstairs. Rob had green eyes, red hair, and was
two eighty, his gut sometimes hung over his
shirt. Denise was helping him with the weight
too. When they met he was almost four hundred.
Denise was the greatest thing that ever
happened to him. There were not words that
could explain how much he loved her, and she
knew it.

When he was walking up the stairs he
didn't see the cat. He stepped on his tail. The
cat screamed as it tried to jump away. Rob did
not get his foot off in time, and when the cat
jumped Rob started to fall backwards, his hands
flew around trying to grab something; he caught
the rail and stopped himself from falling down
the stairs.

"Damn cat, you need to stay off the
stairs," Rob said to himself. When he got to
his room he saw Denise on the bed watching some
lifetime movie like he thought.

"Hi honey, the game over?" asked Denise.

"No, I thought I would just spend time
with you," Rob said.

"Which movie is on?" he continued.

"I don't know the name, something about
gambling."

Right there, Rob should have known
something was wrong right there. Denise always
knew the name of the Lifetime movies that were
on.

"Oh, well I am going to take a shower
first."

A few minutes after Rob went in, the phone
rang.

"Hey Denise, its Kate."

"Kate! Guess what?"

"What?"

"Rob just came upstairs to spend time with
me!"

"And, he is your husband."

"Yeah, but it is the playoffs in football and he left in the middle of the game."

"Wow, I am not married but I know what you mean, my dad and brother are glued to the TV during the playoffs."

"Yeah," she heard the water go off. "I have to go Kate."

"Ok, bye Denise."

"Bye."

When she hung up a black gloved hand flew over her mouth.

"You didn't say anything did you?" said a man from under the bed.

Denise shook her head.

"Good," said the voice.

Then the hand slipped away from Denise's mouth and a man got out from under the bed and started to set something up.

Rob's music was blasting in the bathroom so he heard none of this. When he got out he went to his closet, which was in his bathroom and got dressed. When he opened the door he stopped dead in his tracks.

"What...Who are you, what have you done with my wife?"

Denise was duct taped to a chair in front of a table.

"My name is not important, Rob, you can just call me the dealer," said the man. "Rob, how would you like to play blackjack?"

"I am sorry I don't wan…hey wait, how do you know my name?"

"Not important, just sit down."

Rob sat down.

"Here, have two hundred dollars on me."

Rob's eyes started to gleam. Denise's face showed even more fear, she knew that look.

"I know you will play."

"What?"

"That feeling is coming back, isn't it?

The one that makes you feel invincible. A thing about being addicted to something, you are never cured. Now let's play," said the man.

Rob put in his bet as the man started to deal the cards. Rob peeked at his; a ten and a three.

"Hit me."

The man gave him a King.

"Damn."

Before the next hand the man went under the table and came back up with a shot glass and an open bottle of scotch.

"Smells good doesn't it?"

Rob looked at the bottle, "No, no I am over that."

"Really? Are you sure?" The man poured out a glass and swirled it around and drank it down.

Rob reached behind his back feeling for the gun he kept under his bed.

"Looking for this?" the man asked waving the gun in front of his face.

Rob turned white, "Uh…"

"You try anything like that again, Denise *will* die. Got it?"

"Yes, yes I am sorry."

The man got behind Rob and forced the liquor down his throat. The liquid splashed down, and that was the end of Rob. He grabbed the bottle and chocked it down.

He started to deal out the second hand but Rob was not paying attention. The fear and alcohol had taken over.

"Rob, Rob." The man said snapping his fingers in front of his face.

There was no response.

The man smiled and left the room for a minute. When he left Denise tried to get Robs attention. It was no use-he was gone. Rob turned his head and smiled at her. Denise began to cry. Rob had no idea what was going to happen.

The man came back in and sat back down at the table, "Rob are you ready?" Rob turned back to him in response. "Come here, I want to show you something."

Rob leaned in and the man stabbed his hand to the table.

Rob screamed in pain as he was taken out of trance, he tried to get up when the man stuck his other hand to the table and taped up his mouth. He got on his knees and tied his feet as well as Denise's. He threw an ace of spades on Rob's lap.

The man started to walk out, stopped and looked at Rob and at Denise again and said.

"With the spade you always lose."

"You always lose."

Then he left.

10

Welcome Back Max

"Well?" said Max sitting up straight in his chair.

"Well what?" said David inching closer to the door.

"When were you planning on telling me that the victims were your brother Logan and your future sister-in-law, Ann?"

"Well the thing about that is…"

"Is what, David?" Max said. "Were you just going to keep working this case?"

"I don't see what the big deal is."

"No big deal!" said Max, as his face got redder. "NO BIG DEAL!" he said again, slamming his fists on his desk, making the case file jump. "The big deal is that you are emotionally involved with this case. You could have fucked the whole thing up. When you were working you could be thinking too much about your brother Logan or that Ann and skip right over a piece of evidence, or use the wrong tool and ruin it. Doing that we could have just lost a *very* important piece of evidence, without that, the case goes cold. We really don't need that, our unsolved cases are high enough as it is, and we already lost all of the evidence from the attic. We need all the evidence we can get." Max said. "Now do you see what the big deal is?"

David continued to play it stupid, "OK I

see; I'm sorry."

Max sighed, "Just don't try a stunt like that ever again. Got it?"

"Yes," David said, in an embarrassed voice.

"I'm just glad I found out about this before we went back to the crime scene." Max sat back down in his chair "I don't want to think about what would have happened if Eddie hadn't told me."

After David was gone, Max flipped back open the case folder, and started looking at it again. It was then that Andy came in. Andy was another CSI that worked at the lab, of everyone here Andy had the most experience. He was sixty, gray hair, glasses, and greenish-blue eyes.

"Hey Max."

"Hi."

"How is the case coming?" Andy asked him, moving so he could see the folder."

"Not so good," Max replied.

"Really?" Andy said. "Why?"

"Nothing makes sense; there are no foot prints, no fingerprints, no trace evidence, no nothing. Technically, this murder should not have happened."

"Well you know what, I will try and help you with it later, a new set of eyes always helps."

"Thanks Andy, I really appreciate that."

Then Andy left to let Max work on his case.

After another hour, Max closed the case folder yawning and put it on his desk. Then he got up and stretched, and heard a few joints crack. He decided to take a break now. He was going to walk around the lab a little bit. So he got up and left his office that was not quite organized to his likings yet. He was walking around when he passed David's office, and looked in. David was sitting there staring at the wall like he was in some sort of trance. Max guessed that he was still in shock about the fact that he would never see his brother again. He continued walking until he passed Larry's room. He walked in to say hello.

"Hi Larry."

Larry looked up from the autopsy he was doing.

"Max, long time no see. How are you doing?"

"Good, how are you?"

"Good, Good."

"So," Max said, as he walked over the table the body was on, it was an old man. "How was he killed?"

"You know, I don't just do murders, I have people who died of natural causes too."

"OK," Max said. "How did he die?"

"He had a heart attack, found by wife."

"How did she die?"

"No Max, his wife *found* him."

"Oh, well good seeing you, I need to go; I need to get back to work."

"Ok Max, come back and visit me soon."

Of all the people who worked at the lab, Max was Larry's favorite; he was internally grateful for the work Max did in bringing his wife's killer to justice.

Max then walked into the break room. It had five, three person tables, a fridge, snack and drink machines, and a small TV. He walked over to the snack machine and bought a pack of Lays original potato chips. He sat down at the table closest to the TV and turned it on. He flipped through the channels for a little bit until he found CNN.

Max sat down and watched some of the major headlines. After twenty minutes of news (only three minutes of happy news) Max got up and walked out. He passed by Eddie's lab when he heard someone calling his name.

"Max! Max!"

Max turned around and saw Eddie running out of his lab.

"You...You..." Eddie stopped for a little to catch his breath. "You're not going to believe this. The knife that killed Logan also killed Ann."

"What? Max said surprised. I thought we lost all the evidence when I was stabbed."

"Well, apparently some blood got in the little cracks of the handle and the fire skipped over it. So..." he said, handing a paper to Max. "I tested it and two mixed readings came back. So I put it in the centrifuge and when it finished, the two samples were both our victims." Eddie said.

How did he manage to kill the female, that knife was fairly normal?" Eddie asked.

"I don't know, maybe some splatter just got caught." Max took the paper and walked back to his office. "Thanks Eddie." He called.

"No problem."

When Max got there he opened the case file and put in the only known piece of evidence.

As soon as Max sat back down in his office David rushed in.

"Max!"

"What is it, David? I have a lot of work to do."

"We have another case."

"Another one?" said Max. "What happened at this one?"

"It's another murder; the MO looks the same-double, husband and wife, and there are knife marks on the arms."

"Another one? Shit." Max said. "Oh well, might as well try this one. We are just getting a big goose egg from here."

"So will this one just run cold?"

"Oh no, I will just give it to Andy and Ken, they are pretty good, maybe they can solve it."

"Doubt it," David said. "You are the best we have"

"I know that, but they might see something I did not," Max said. "You have got to have more faith in your co-workers."

"Yeah, you are right, might as well give them a chance."

"Good, that's a better attitude." Max said.

Max went into his desk and got a paper and a pen then he wrote why he could not work the case anymore, and how much it meant to him that they pick up this case; he attached it to the case file with a paperclip. Then he followed David out tossing the file on Andy's desk as he passed.

11

Found

When David and Max got to the parking lot, they decided to take David's car, because Max's was nearly out of gas and might not make the trip to the crime scene, back to the lab then home. David had made that mistake before, he broke down on a one hundred and twenty degree day, and the evidence had been fried. He would not make it again.

Since they were not taking Max's car, he went over it to get his gear. He jumped to the bed of his truck and went to the sliver tool box that was built in the back. When he got to it, he took a little key out of his pocket and opened it. The inside was specially insolated like a cooler so the heat would not destroy his gear or any evidence. There was three silver suitcases with black handles. Two looked brand new; they were spotless and shimmered in the sun. The third had several rust stains and no longer shimmered. Max picked that one, under it was his bullet proof vest. It was black with white stripes built on the neck. On the right side there was a little pocket with Levinton stitched on in little white letters, clipped to the inside of the pocket was his ID. On the back was LAS VEGAS CRIME LAB in big white letters. He slipped it on, the vest stopped at his waist and his shoulders. Then he closed his tool box and locked it. He walked over to David and they went over to his Corvette and got in.

When Max got in, he put his case with all
his tools in it on the ground, buckled up, and
flipped on some blue Oakley's. David looked at
Max as he started the car.

"Why do you have that on already?" David
asked. "We won't be at the crime scene for
about fifteen minutes.

"You never know when a murderer has been
keeping an eye on you, so I never take it off
until I get home."
"Were you wearing it the night you got
stabbed?"

"Yeah I-I was, but the-the um suspect from
your brother's, case. He stabbed me right where
the vest ends, see?" Max said, still uneasy
about his close call with death.

Max rolled up his sleeve revealing a big
white wrap that went under his shirt.

"Does that wrap go around you whole body?"

"Yeah, it is a real bitch, I can hardly
move without stretching the crap out of my
skin. I can't even take it off, I have to put
saran wrap around it when I take a shower."

"That sucks," said David, as he too
flipped on some Oakley's, his were silver.

"Let's go," David stepped on the gas so
hard the speed threw Max back to his seat. Max
was holding on for dear life as David sped out
of the parking lot.

"Whoa, easy David, you do *know* about a
little thing called the *speed limit.*"

"Yeah, I know," he said, slowing down the
car. "I just wanted to show you how fast this
baby goes."

Max looked at him wide-eyed.

"Hey us old guys know how to have fun
too." David said.

Max laughed uneasily and took a firm hold
on the *oh-shit* handle. Then they set off in the
direction of their newest crime scene.

When they arrived at the crime scene there were four Clarke County police cars outside with their lights flashing-the yellow CRIME SCENE tape was already up. Max got out while David went to the back seat to get his tools. He came back with a silver case much like the other ones in Max's truck. Then he put on his bullet proof vest. It looked just like Max's except his said Walker on the front pocket. When he was all set he walked over to Max, it was then that he noticed the old case in his hands.

"Why do you keep that old thing?" David asked.

"Good luck," Max said. "These are the tools I used to collect the murder from the Orange Creek killings."

"Reeeeallly," David said, quite a bit surprised. "Don't you need to update your tools?"

"Oh I have, I just keep the case."

"Whatever," David said as they went towards the yellow CRIME SCENE DO NOT CROSS tape. David lifted it up and Max ducked under, David did the same, and they made their way to the door.

"Hey wait!" Max and David turned around to see a young looking cop probably not even old enough to drink yet. "You can't be here."

Max and David both flashed their badges "Las Vegas Crime Lab."

"Oh sorry," said the cop in an embarrassed voice. "Go right ahead."

When they entered the house David said. "What a moron, didn't he see Las Vegas Crime Lab on our backs in big enough letters that Stevie Wonder could see."

"I know they don't set standards high enough these days."

They glanced around the entrance, until a

cop motioned them upstairs. They walked up to
the room the cop was standing by, went in and
gasped.

There was a man that was leaned over a
poker table that was covered in blood and
vomit. Beside the bed a women lay in a chair
with vomit around the edges of the tape that
was covering her mouth. Max walked over to the
table and reached for the man's head.

David grabbed his hand "No Max, we can't
touch the body until Larry checks them out and
does an autopsy.

"What happened here?" Max asked the cop.

"We d-don't know we...we came to check
this p-place out because of a noise complaint
and..." the man took a breath.

Max did not let him finish. "Is this your
first time on body watch?"

"Ya...yes." The man gagged.

"Go, Go."

The cop ran out covering his mouth.
Another came in and looked back at his partner.
"Rookies," the new cop said. He covered his
mouth. "God, how do you get used to that
smell?"

"Years and years," replied David.

"Vic's Vapor Rub," Max said, pointing to
his shiny upper lip. "It blocks the smell."

"I guess he held out pretty well
considering the circumstances," said the new
cop.

"Yeah he did," said Max, thinking about
what had happened when he saw David's brother
for the first time.

"OK, now again, how did this happen?"

"Like my partner was trying to say, we got
the call because neighbors complained of a bad
smell and feared the worst. When we came in we
found this," the cop said.

"Wait, you touched the TV?"

"Well yes bu..."

"Why? You never touch anything in the scene."

"Sorry sir."

"Just don't do it again, did you touch anything else?"

"No."

While Max was talking to the cop David was busy taking pictures of the scene.

"One more question, did you call the coroner yet?"

"Yes, he did."

Max turned around and saw Larry coming in.

"Oh, hey Larry."

"Hey Max, didn't think I'd see you at a scene so soon," he said. "I thought you were working on David's brother's case."

"Oh yeah, I gave that to Andy and Ken."

"Oh alright," said Larry. He looked back and saw David. "Hi David."

"Hey Larry," said David, without taking his face out of the camera. "I am almost done with the pictures; you can have the bodies soon."

After a few more flashes, David put the camera away, "Alright, they are all yours."

Larry snapped on some latex gloves and went over to the male body and started to check it out. He stopped almost as soon as he had started.

"Did you move the body at all?"

"No sir," said the cop.

"Why, what happened?" asked Max

"Come here you guys, you have to see this."

Max and David snapped on some latex gloves as well, and joined Larry by the male body. Max and David just sat there clueless on what Larry had seen.

Larry sighed, "Look here; look at the

force marks on the arm." He pointed to the bruises, he was moved around forcefully, maybe even after death."

"Look at where it was," Max said. "It looks like it was blocking the mans pocket."

Larry looked at Max, "You still got it."

"Thanks."

"OK, back to the body; if the arm was moved, the killer must have wanted something. Look, the arm was blocking his pocket." Larry moved the arm again and reached in the pocket and took out a wallet. There was no ID or credit cards. "No ID or anything that can tell us who he was." Then Larry went over to the female, by her chair was a purse. He reached in and took out her pocket book. Then he opened it and sighed. "No ID or credit cards here either." Then Larry went back to the male to check for trace. Max and David kneeled beside him to watch.

"Ned, 'ell them crime scene 'eople to com ere, I fink I ound somthin portant," said a familiar voice from the hall.

Max got up at the sound and looked at the door "No, it can't be."

He walked out of the room and into the hallway, stopped dead in his tracks and sighed. "Ah shit,."

There standing in the hall in all of his glory was Chief Victor Powell.

"Ruke, that ou?"

"I am not your "ruke" any more, Powell."

The Chief grunted.

"What was it you wanted to show me?"

"'ook over ere, there be part missin from them photos."

Max looked over, at the vast wall of pictures and saw that some parts had been cut out.

"David, you might want to come see this."

David walked over and looked in the direction of Max's finger.

"Look at the pictures, every other person is cut out except for the victims," Max said. "Our killer does not want us to know something."

"That must mean that our victims are important, or know someone important," David said.

"Thanks for this Powell," said Max as he went back to the room and got the camera; he took pictures of the wall then went back to the room. Larry was leaving with the bodies.

"Alright boys, the scene is all yours," Larry said. "Sorry I did not find any trace evidence on the bodies."

"Don't worry about it," Max said. "That is not your job, we just need to know how and when they died."

"I think hey have been dead for two weeks."

"Really?" David asked. "How do you know?"

"There is a day calendar in there, the last date on it is the third of January, now it is the seventeenth, but some people forget to take some off and based on the level of decomp. But you can never trust those so I will let you know for sure after the autopsy."

"Good going Larry," Max said. "Now we have an estimate of the time of death."

Then Larry left.

Max and David walked into the room getting ready to collect evidence. They first dusted around the table for fingerprints, (there was none,) then Max took samples of the blood on the table just to make sure some of it was not the killer's. He put it in a test tube then labeled it. He and David got on the floor and started to look for evidence that the killer may have accidentally dropped. They searched over the whole floor and found nothing.

They both sat down by the door.

"Damn, nothing!" said David.

"Yeah nothing, this is just like the last cas..." Max trailed off.

"Max?" David called. "Max, what's wrong?"

Max just kept looking forward, like in a trance.

"Max!"

"Huh, what?"

"Are you OK?" David asked again. "You left me for a second."

"Oh, that, come here, I will show you."

David went over to where Max was sitting.

"Now," Max said, as he positioned David at the angle he was at. "Crouch your head a little down and look at that table."

David did as he was told, "I don't see anything."

"Come here," Max said walking over to the table. He took out a Q-tip and ran it over the throw up. The Q-tip made a small rise and drop near the middle-David gasped.

Max just smiled.

"Damn, you're good," said David.

"You see, there is something under the blood."

Max went over and got out a little knife. He put it down on the table. Max lowered his face just above the surface and began to cut.

"Oh shit," Max said. "I don't like the shape that this is taking."

David could not see the cut, but he knew what Max was talking about, "Let's hope we aren't right."

Max finished cutting and flipped it, "Shit."

"Is it really?" David asked.

"Yep," Max said, flipping the object to show him, "Another ace of spades."

12

A Swarm of Parasites

"Another?" David asked.

"Yep, our killer has struck again," Max said, as he took a picture and bagged the ace. "Let's look around again in case he got sloppy."

Max and David crouched down and started to look for anything that the killer may have left behind. While they were on their way back to the door David put his hand in some dried blood. Frightened, he pulled it back as he did he pulled a hair out of the blood.

"Max," David called holding up the hair still partially stuck in the blood. "Could you bring me the camera, I found something.

Max went over and got the camera, brought it to the bed, and handed it to David. David put the hair back down beside an evidence marker. He snapped it a few times, and then handed it back to Max.

"What did you find?" Max asked.

"It's a blonde hair, most likely female-what color is the victims?"

Max got up and checked the notes, "Brown."

David pulled himself up, and bagged the hair, "As it turns out the killer is human. Let's see what else we have." David got back down around the bed area, "Bingo."

"What?"

"It looks like a tiny piece of leather."

"A piece of leather, what color?" Max said in a suspecting voice.

"Black,"

"We found a piece of black leather in your brother's attic, snagged on a nail, remember?"

"Yeah," David said in a far away voice.

"But why did we find some here?" Max said, as he put the evidence away. "There was nothing for it to have caught on."

"Wait!" David said, with mild excitement. "Didn't you say that after the killer stabbed you he burned the evidence?"

"Yeah," Max said.

"Maybe he took the leather..."

"And planted it under the bed," Max finished.

"Yep, just what I was thinking," David said. "He is playing a game with us, a very sick mind game."

"I don't think we will get much more from here," David concluded. "Would you like to call it?"

"Love to," Max said. "The way I see it, our killer was under the bed at some point based on the leather you found-he may have even hidden under it. If that is the case then that means that he was waiting here for his victims. When you think about that he must have found a way in when they were away-probably the same way he managed to get in and out of your brothers house. The male must have been somewhere, maybe not in the room yet when the wife was tied to the chair. When he came to the room he was forced to do something with that table." Max said, looking around the room seeing it in his mind's eye. "He made them think that he might let them go if they do something. Then he stole their IDs making sure we did not know who they are. I'm still not sure why he cut the photos though."

David smiled, "done?"

Max sighed with relief. "It felt so good to do." Max looked around further examining the room when he saw a glint on the table. He stared at it for a moment when the sun disappeared behind the clouds. Max could not seem to find it again. So he got an instant camera out again and took a picture of the spot he saw the glint. When the picture came out the glint was in it. Max stared hard at the picture to see the spot.

"What are you doing?" asked David.

Max just handed him the picture as he went to the spot with some tweezers.

"Hey, what's this glint?" asked David.

Max came up with a piece of glass that was half covered in blood. It was clear and had a little piece of paper on it. Max turned it around a few times.

"Morgan," Max said reading the label. "He got them drunk, that way he could get things from them easier. They had no idea what was going on," Max said putting the glass in an evidence bag.

"Now that we have finished the main crime scene, let's take a closer look at those pictures," David said as they went in the hall towards the pictures.

"Well, on the bright side this time we have a picture to put on the news to get names sooner," Max said.

For the amount of evidence that was in the room there was even less outside.

"Wow, this guy is good. There is nothing here to tell us who these people are, who they knew that made them so important, and there nothing to tell us who this guy is." David said.

Max reached down to his waist and got his

pager. He pushed the button and saw the message-"Andy???????"-come up.

"What does that mean?" David asked looking over.

"He must be confused about the case I left on his desk." Max said as he flipped open his phone and dilled Andy.

He answered after one ring, "Shepard."

"Hey Andy, you got a question for me?" Max asked.

"Yes, I was looking for you, what's with the case on my desk?"

"That, we could not do anything with that, we hardly found anything at the scene, what we did find was destroyed, and the pictures came up empty."

"Alright, I will give it a try, I'll take Ken with me, he could use training like this," Andy said. "Where are you now?"

"Oh, I got a new case, I am at the crime scene right now, David is with me," Max told him. "And I just found another ace of spades so we are technically working the same case."

"Alright, well I am heading out to the crime scene right now. I will let you know if I find anything."

"Good luck Andy."

"Thanks.".

"Well, it looks like there is no trace, but we better double check just in case," David said.

"Well, there is no trace on the floor around the pictures, but maybe he left himself on the frames."

Max went and got the fingerprint dust and when he came back they began to dust the frames. Not one print showed up.

"Shit," David said "The bastard wiped them clean."

"Should have seen that coming," Max said.

"Well at least we still have the DNA from the hairs that I found under the bed," David said.

Max checked his watch "We should stop for the day and try and get a head start on the lab work."

"OK," David said. "We have been here a couple hours. Damn, time flies when you really get in to this job. Tomorrow we will do the perimeter."

"And then we will try to find what cut those pictures." Max finished for him.

By now Max and David were back in the main hall of the house. They walked to the door and opened it, and were greeted by light brighter than the sun. It seemed to them that they had died and were at the pearly gates. They covered their eyes and walked forward into the wall of light. When they were through it they saw the source of it- the Press. They were everywhere, the road around was filled with news vans and there had to be at least fifty reporters waiting on the other side of the tape.

"Oh great, the press is here," Max said with deep sarcasm. "the never ending swarm of parasites that attaches itself to a story and kills and ruins everything about it. Then, not caring about anything that happened, they move on to the next story, leaving the old one dead in the dust." Max shook his head, ashamed. "Then the violent cycle repeats itself every day."

As Max and David neared the Corvette the reporters rushed toward them. "Mr. Levinton, Mr. Levinton-Mr. Walker, Mr. Walker," shouted many different male and female voices. "What can you tell us about the investigation so far?"

"Not much," David muttered, keeping his head out of the pictures the best he could.

"Mr. Walker, does the fact that this is the same killer that struck just about two months ago change anything?"

"What?" David said, suddenly not caring how many head shots got on the news. "Who told you that?"

They turned to Max, ignoring David's question.

"Mr. Levinton, how does it feel to be after the same man who stabbed you just about two months ago?"

"Where are you and how are you getting all this?" Max, now as angry as David, yelled.

They ignored Max as well.

"So about this case, what can you tell us?"

"Good God!" David screamed, dropping his evidence suitcase. He took out a picture of the victims and pushed it in their faces. "Here, you happy? This is a picture of our victims; put it on your shitty little news station. See if anyone recognizes them."

Cameras flashed everywhere. Before they began to ask more questions Max and David managed to sneak back into David's car.

"Wow, I really blew up," David said ashamed.

"David, don't worry, they can really get to you," Max said, with remorse. "Really, how do you think they got that information? You know, about our two cases being connected."

"I think one of those cops at the scene shared that little information. They must have seen you find the ace."

"Sounds plausible."

"Damn-Damn-Damn-Damn-DAMN!" David screamed, slamming his hands down on the steering wheel. "I still cannot believe I blew up like that."

"David, forget about it, it's over, there

is nothing you can do to change it. You did a
good job holding down your anger, you just
released it at the wrong time,"

    "I know, I know, but this will be all over
the news tonight, tomorrow, tomorrow night, and
who knows how long. I can see the headlines
now: "CSI David Walker exploded at the press
today; this behavior is very uncalled for and
has launched a state investigation of the lab."
That's it , that is how it will happen. My
career will be ruined."

    "No one who cares about your abuse of the
press will even remember this in a week. They
will already be on the next 'big thing' by
tonight" Max said, trying to comfort David.
"The violent cycle repeats itself every day."
Max took a deep breath and shook his head,
still ashamed. "It happens every day."

13

The New Team

"Ken! Ken!" Andy called as he walked through the halls of the lab. "Where is that kid?" he said to himself. "Ken!"

"What?" said a dazed and confused voice in the distance. Andy followed it and found Ken in the lab with Eddie.

"Ken, I have a new case and I want you to come with me," Andy said. "You could use the training. Max handed it down to us."

"Wait," Ken said. "You mean Max. The Max Levinton? The Orange Creek Max?"

"None other," Andy replied.

"No disrespect to you sir, but if Max could not find anything, then there is no way in hell that we can."

"Rookie, Rookie, Rookie," Andy said shaking his head. "Do you remember Max's first case?"

"Orange Creek," Ken said "Are you kidding, I studied it in college."

"It was that case that brought Max's name out, it made him famous," Andy said. "After that, everyone wanted him to solve their crimes."

"Yeah, I know about that too."

"Well, the person that handed it down to Max's old supervisor was among the best in the nation. Max was just a trainee, like you. He solved it and three years later he was on top of the world."

"No, I did not hear about that part."

"Did you ever think that you could be the next Max?"

Ken got very excited at this. "OK sir, let me get my tools."

When they got to Logan and Ann's house they went to the floor below the attic.

"Shouldn't we be up there?"

"No, Max and David already did that; we will be looking at the space around the main crime scene."

They began to look around the trap door leading to the attic. Andy took samples of the plaster, meanwhile, Ken dusted for prints.

"Now, don't be surprised if Max's prints show up. He discovered the scene when he was with the Clarke County Police." Andy saw that Ken was clueless. "Last year David was given evidence implicating Max in a scandal. David quickly fired him in response and because of the extremity of the circumstances Max was unable to find a job in investigation."

"So why is he back now?"

"Well, David's source turned out to be bad and now we have our man back."

Andy looked down at his feet sighing. "Max was right, this guy is good." It was then that Andy noticed the muddy foot prints. They were barely noticeable but they were there. Andy followed them, as did Ken, although Ken did not know what was going on. The prints led them to the kitchen.

They both started to scan the kitchen. The footprints led to the dishwasher. Andy walked in and took a picture of the dishwasher. There was something inside-beeping.

"What is it?" Andy asked.

"I don't know." Ken said. "There is something inside beeping." Ken took another picture and reached out to open it.

Its something beeping he had said, *something beeping.* Bombs beeped-Bombs. It was a bomb.

"Ken NO!" Andy screamed running toward him. "It's a..."

Andy was too late; Ken had opened the dishwasher and set off the bomb. They were both blown away-along with the crime scene.

14

A New Level of Fe♠r

When Max and David arrived back at the crime lab, David made a case folder, while Max dropped the trace evidence off at Eddie's lab. Then they walked back to the parking lot and went their separate ways.

When David got back to his condo, he noticed that the door was locked; he never locked the door when he had company. Something was wrong, and David had a bad feeling about it.

"Mom!" David yelled, slamming his fists on the door. "Mom! Open up!" David paused for a little to listen to find out if anyone was coming. He could hear the faint sound of sobbing.

David took out his keys and tried to open the door, but he couldn't turn his key. David began to panic-something was *very* wrong.

"Mom! Please open up!" He put his head to the door again waiting for an answer or for it to open, neither came. All he could hear was the faint sound of sobbing.

"Damn it," David said, slamming his hand against the wall. He stepped back and crossed himself. Then he raced forward and kicked his

door down. The frame shattered and the door
swung open. David's mom was on the floor
crying; there was a note beside her.

At that time he heard the window slam
shut. David could just barely make out the
outline of a person. He ran over to the window
and looked out. He saw a man in a trench coat
and a cowboy hat. He was jumping over the rails
easily landing on the next. It looked like he
had super human reflexes just like Max had
said. David walked back over to his mom and
picked up the note. It was an ace of spades. He
was right; the Spade knew who he was. The Spade
was in his house. Then he noticed that there
was some writing on it. David turned on a light
to read it.

**D♠vid, how ♠re you? I s♠w that M♠x
m♠n♠ged to survive my little visit. I ♠m quite
sure that you will not. I do not w♠nt to hurt
your mom, I w♠nt you, I w♠nt M♠x ♠nd the rest
of you little pricks th♠t work ♠t th♠t crime
l♠b. I sh♠ll see you soon!**

When Max got home he went to the kitchen,
Sue was getting dinner ready. She was making
London broil, just the smell of the marinade
was overwhelming-in a good way. It made the
whole kitchen smell delightful. Sue never
admitted or bragged about it, but she had to be
one of the greatest amateur chefs ever. Max was
not afraid though, he knew of his wife's
cooking skills, and was happy to brag. Just
about every day, Max would bring the leftovers
for lunch, one of the ways he showed off
without coming right out and saying it.

"Hi, sweetie," Max said, kissing his wife.
"How was your day?"

"It was good," Sue said, as she put the

London broil in the oven. "How about you?"

"It was okay," Max said. "I got a new case today, and it is linked to my old one." Max stopped because Sue looked clueless. "The case I had on my first day back; the one where the suspect stabbed me."

"Oh, that case," Sue said. "But you're not supposed to tell me about your cases, are you?"

"No, but you would have found out tonight anyway, it's going to be all over the news," Max said.

"Oh, why?" Sue asked.

"It's a long story really, why don't you sit down and I'll tell you," Max said, as they sat down on the couch..

"So, this guy has killed four people now, do you think this could be another Orange Creek?"

"Oh, God I hope not," Max said. "Where are the boys?"

"I think they are at a friend's house," Sue said getting a little closer to Max.

"Hi!" said two voices that came from the front porch.

"Or, they could be home," Sue said, as she and Max got off the couch to get ready for dinner.

"Hey dad," Bill said. "Some man outside told me to give this to you." Bill handed Max an envelope.

"Let me see that," Max said, reaching for the envelope.

Max ripped it open and dumped the contents of it into his hand. It was an ace of spades; there was writing on it.

Hi Max! I see you managed to make it through my little visit. I don't think you will be as lucky next time. I do not want to hurt your wife or kids. I want you, I want David, and the rest of you little pricks that work at

th♠t crime l♠b. I sh♠ll see you soon!!

Max just let it drop to the floor. "Max what wrong?" Sue asked.

"Nothing, everything is just fine."

Max walked over to Bill, "Bill, what did this man look like?"

"Well," Bill said, thinking. "He was tall, and he had a trench coat, a cowboy hat, and some black leather gloves."

"Oh, okay thanks," he said as the color drained from his face.

When there was about five minutes left before the London broil was done, Max's cell phone started to ring.

He picked it up, and walked to the other room, "Levinton." Max answered.

"Max!" said David, with fear in his voice.

Max sensed it and replied, "David, what's wrong?"

"The Spade sent me a note today."

"Did you get one too?"

"An ace of spades with a little note on it," David said.

"My God, David do you know what this means?"

"He knows where we live."

"Holy shit, we might need to call in some extra help on this one."

"I was thinking the same thing," David said. "Let's talk about it more at the autopsy tomorrow."

"Alright, see you then."

Max then walked back to the kitchen, dinner was ready.

After a filling dinner, Max and Sue made some coffee and sat down to watch the news, before it started the blue emergency screen came on and instructed them to turn to channel thirteen. Max picked up the changer and turned to channel thirteen. Soon after, the blue screen turned to the breaking news. It was a picture of the remains of a house that looked like it had burned down, shown from a helicopter's point of view.

"At about five pm today, this house, an open crime scene, exploded. According to our sources, two crime scene investigators were in the house at the time of the explosion. At this time we do not know their identities. Stay with us as we keep you informed on this developing story."

As the screen went back to blue, before going back to the regular scheduled programming, Max dropped his coffee cup. When it hit the floor it didn't just shatter, it exploded. Pieces went all over the living room.

"Max, what's wrong?" Sue said.

"I think that that's the crime scene that I gave to Andy and Ken," Max said. "This should not have happened, that should have been me, and they should not have died."

"Max, sweaty, there was nothing you could have done. How many thousands of crime scenes are investigated every year? You had no way of knowing that something like this would or even could happen."

"Yeah, I know it's just..." Max sighed and went outside. Sue let him be alone.

The next morning when Max was getting ready for work his fears were realized, when they had identified the bodies as Andy and Ken.

When Max arrived at work he was surprised to see that there were not that many cars in the parking lot. It must have been earlier than he thought. Which was good. Max hoped that Larry would be ready, so the autopsies would be done soon. Then Max would have some quiet time, to think about the case, and other things. Max

liked silence, it created the best environment
for him. He could hear every little thing that
was going on around him. He liked to sit back
in his chair and close his eyes. He tried to
recreate the case that way. It would look very
weird to anyone else. He also moved his hand
around like it was the killer's. As Max opened
the door, he gave a little extra prayer that
the autopsies would be finished early. He liked
silence.

Max dropped off his things and headed down
to Larry's domain. Right before he went in he
stopped by the door and slipped on a white lab
coat and some latex gloves. Then he got some
Vic's Vapor Rub, and rubbed it on his upper
lip. In all his years he still had never gotten
used to the smell of dead bodies. He would not
have made it as a CSI if he had not found out
about vapor rub. It blocked out all smells so,
he would not throw up, like he did with Logan.
He did not know how Larry could stand it, Max
would die if he had to be around dead bodies
all day. He put the Vic's back in his pocket,
took a deep breath to make sure that was all he
could smell. Then he pushed open the metal
doors and went to his first autopsy all year.

It felt so good to be back.

15

The Autopsies (II)

When Max entered, Larry was getting the bodies ready and David was standing by the tables waiting.

"Hey, Max did anything else happen last night, with the um...?" David looked over and saw that Larry had gone back to the freezer to get the other body. "With The Spade?"

"No, thank God for that," Max said. "What about you?" he asked.

"Well, did I tell you how The Spade had a gun in my house?"

"No, I don't think so."

"Well, after I called you I notified the FBI-they should be here by the end of the week."

"Alright that sounds good," Max said. "Wait, About what time did The Spade leave your house?"

"I would have to say about...six o'clock."

"Shit, I was afraid of that."

"What?" David said.

"You live about ten minutes to the east of here right?"

"Yeah, right down the street," David said.

"Well, I live about thirty minutes to the west depending on the traffic." Max said. "And I got my note at about six fifteen."

"What?" David said. "So there are two?"

"Yep," Max said. The Spade is two."

"What's two?" Larry said, as he rolled out

the male body.

"Nothing, just the case we are doing," Max
said. "There are two people."

"Oh, like a partnership." Larry said in
his cheerful voice.

"Sure...that's um...one way to put it,"
Max said in an uneasy shaky voice. "So, are you
ready to start the autopsy?" Max asked,
regaining his composure.

"Sure, Max," Larry said. "Are you ready to
start, David?"

David flashed a thumbs up, "Sure let's do
it...wait a minute."

"What?" Larry said.

"What's that scar down his chest?" David
asked.

"His file says that he recently had a
double bypass," Larry said, showing David.

"Oh, OK," David said. "That just looked a
little fishy."

"You don't need to worry," Larry said, a
little mad. "I would know if something was
wrong with one of my bodies."

"Sorry."

"Just don't do it again."

"Ok," David said.

"Alright," Larry said, as he slipped on
some goggles. "Let's do it." Larry picked up
the scalpel and Max and David slipped on some
goggles of their own.

David and Max leaned in as Larry made the
first slit from the right shoulder down to the
chest, and then did the same from the left.
Then he cut one long slit down to the waist; he
pulled back the skin up and clamped it into
place.

"Alright, so far everything looks normal,"
Larry said. "Let's take a look at the internal
organs." He got out the saw to cut through the
rib bones. The second he put the saw on the

ribs they broke.

"Whoa!" All three of them said at the same time.

"What the hell!" Max said.

"In my forty-one years as a coroner, I have never seen something like this."

"Why did they break?" David asked.

"I don't know, let me check," Larry said, as he went and got a magnifying glass. He came back and tilted his head in towards the ribs. He held on to the side of the table for balance. Suddenly, Max and David saw Larry's grip on the table increase greatly.

"Larry," David said, as he and Max looked down into the body. "Larry, what's wrong?"

David saw Max get back up, trying to hold back puke. "Sorry, Sorry," he said, waving his hand as the urge wore off. "Larry?" Max said, going back to the body without leaning back in. "Are you okay?"

Larry finally got back up. "Um...David, Max you um... you might want to take a look at this."

Max went first. He took the magnifying glass and leaned down into the body. After about thirty seconds, David leaned back up. "Um...Yeah," Max turned back to David. "You might want to take a look at this."

David took the magnifying glass from Max, took a deep breath and leaned down into the body.

"Check out the lungs." Larry said

David looked down at the lungs which had something carved in them. David put the magnifying glass over the carvings and reveled a message. The left side of the lung read:

Four down-four down.
The ultimate end is sooner than you know.
One of you will pay-one of you will pay.

"The end is near, one of you will pay."
David said, "What the hell is going on?"

"Larry?" Max said as he saw him shaking.
"We can finish this later if you want to."

"No," Larry said steadying himself. "No,
let's finish this up now," Larry put his hands
in and pulled out the heart. As he did,
something burst and blood sprayed all over Max.

Max gasped in fear, and suddenly felt very
faint. He tried to stabilize himself as the
feeling came on stronger and stronger. After a
few seconds, Max lost the fight against
gravity. He started to fall backwards, arms
flying wildly at his sides. As he saw the
ceiling get farther and farther away, he could
see David and Larry running towards him. They
were too late, Max's head bounced off the floor
with a sickening thud, and everything went
black.

16

Expect the Unexpected

"Maaaaaax. Maaaaaax." Max could hear someone calling him, but he did not recognize the voice. He stood up and looked around, everything was black. Max felt a lump form in his stomach. Where was he?

"Turn around Max." The voice said, in a commanding but soothing voice. Max turned around and saw The Spade looking right at him. His face was hidden under the shadow of the cowboy hat that he always wore. "Hi Max," said The Spade, lifting one finger in a raise. "I told you I would see you soon." Max froze in fear. He watched helplessly as The Spade rushed towards him, knife in hand. At full speed The Spade shoved the knife into Max's stomach and thrust it up. Max screamed in pain as The Spade looked down into his eyes. Max could feel himself slipping away. The Spade's face was still shadowed, but Max could hear him starting to laugh. With the strength he had left Max reached up and pulled off The Spade's hat and saw David.

"Max wake up!" he yelled in David's voice. "Wake up Max!"

Suddenly The Spade and the pain vanished. The darkness started to slowly fade away and Max could see a blurred version of the ceiling and two heads looking down at him. All of a

sudden it made sense. He was at work when blood
had sprayed all over him. There had been
something else too, something about the body,
but he could not remember.

As his vision started to improve, Max
started to get up, when he felt a firm hand on
his shoulder gently pushing him back down. "You
need to take it easy, let us help you," Larry
said, as he grabbed Max's left hand, and David
grabbed the other. As he was lifted up, Max
felt a huge jolt of pain shoot up his back and
explode in his head. The pain was so great that
Max tried to rip his hands out of Larry's and
David's, luckily they had a firm grip on his
hands or he would have gone back down.

"Easy, Max," Larry said, as they helped
him into a chair. "You took quite a fall."
Suddenly the aftermath of the fall hit Max full
blast and he felt like he was going to puke.
Larry must have sensed it too, because he put a
bucket in his lap.

"Thank you," Max said, as David gave him
an ice pack. Max looked up at David "And thank
you too."

"Max," Larry said. "I am going to check
you out a little to make sure you are OK."
Larry continued as he shined a light in each of
Max's eyes. "Seems alright, now Max, how many
fingers am I holding up?"

"Three," Max said, in a queasy voice.

"Yep, very good."

When Larry went into the other room Max
put the ice pack on his head. When he first put
it on the pain was extravagant again. Then, the
ice numbed the pain a little, but not too much.

David pulled a chair in front of Max.
"Max?" he said. "Do you remember what
happened?"

"Kind of."

"Well," David said. "We had just started

the autopsy when the ribs snapped. Then Larry went to see what had happened, and there was a note on the lungs. When we went back to continue the autopsy Larry had just pulled back the ribs and something exploded and blood flew all over you and….well you can guess the rest."

"Here Max," Larry said, handing Max a fizzing glass and some pills. Max looked up at him still dazed. "Here is some Tylenol for the pain, and some Sprite to ease your stomach."

"Thank you," Max said, as he took the pills and started to sip on the Sprite. "Do I have a-"

Larry finished for him. "A concussion? I think you do, that was quite a nasty fall you took, and I must insist that you see a doctor-as soon as possible. Actually you should see one today."

"Alright," Max said, finishing the Sprite and getting his cell phone. Max scrolled down until he saw his doctor's number, and dialed it. After a few rings, he picked up. Max gave him some minor details, and made the appointment.

"Alright," Max said. "I need to go home, I have a four o'clock appointment." He looked at David. "Can you finish the autopsy by yourself? And try to find out more about that note thing?"

"Sure, Sure," David said. "And I will go to Eddie's lab too."

"Yeah, that a good idea," Larry said. "He is probably waiting for the samples that I am taking from the bodies."

"Alright, I am going to call my wife, because I don't fell safe driving home

"Good idea, its better to play it safe." Larry said.

Max dialed up his wife who picked up after two rings.

"Hello?"

"Hey, honey," Max said. "I got hurt at work again."

Max's wife gasped. "What happened?"

"Well it's kind of complicated," Max said. "We were in the middle of the autopsy, when some blood sprayed on me. Then I fainted, I hit my head pretty hard."

"Ouch," Sue said sympathetically. "Sounds painful."

"It is very painful," Max replied. "And I think that I have a concussion too. I already made an appointment, and don't want to take a risk driving."

"Ok," she said. "What time?"

"Four."

"Alright, I am on my way."

"Ok, see you soon hon."

Max hung up his phone, and sat back in his chair as Larry and David finished the autopsies. About thirty minutes later, Sue showed up. She talked to Larry and David for a few minutes. Then Larry helped Max get back to the car, while David walked down to Eddie's lab.

As David was walking down to Eddie's lab, his cell phone started to ring. He picked it up on the second ring.

"Walker."

"Hi David, how have you been doing?"

David started to answer "Go...wait w-who is this?"

"Don't you want to know how I have been doing, David?" the man said.

"Who is this?" David said, a little more stern.

"Come on David, don't be rude now."

David sighed. "How are you doing?"

"That's more like it," the man said. "I am doing fine."

"Now, who are you?" David said, starting to lose his patience.

"No, David it's not time for that yet. I want you to just keep walking; don't go into Eddie's lab."

David froze. "What?"

"I said, do not go to Eddie's lab, just keep walking," the man repeated.

"H-How do you know where I am going."

"You ask too many questions, David." The man said a little annoyed. "Just keep walking past Eddie's lab and go back to your office."

"And what if I don't?" David said, with a little smirk. "What if I just hang up right now, and go to Eddie's lab."

"Oh, I don't think you want to know what would happen if you did that, David," The man said, now very annoyed.

David stopped and leaned against the wall. "Just humor me," he said. "What would happen?"

The man spoke slowly and softly, when he finished David was too horrified to speak. He just stood there against the wall with his mouth wide open.

"You don't need to talk now. Just leave those samples where you are and go to your office."

David let the samples drop from his hand and he started to walk towards his office.

"David, I am curious about something."

"What is it?"

"How come Max is the best CSI you have, and he can't handle a little blood?"

"Wh-what, how do you know about that?"

"How do I know?" the man asked. "I thought you would have figured that out by now," he said with a chuckle. "I am like the wind, David, I am everywhere you go, but you can neither see nor catch me."

David took a breath and held back his urge to scream, and answered the question. "I don't know really, since he was a rookie, he has never been too good with it."

"Oh yes Max's rookie year. I remember his first case. Orange Creek. Boy, that was a big case, and a little rookie like him solved it."

"Yep," David said. "The start of the Max Levinton era."

"Start of an era, my ass. That little prick put my best friend to death."

"He should not have killed fifteen people," David said.

"You take that back, it was not his fault. It was your little friend, Max's. You take it back right now or your life is over. Right now. I can take it right now."

"S-Sorry," David said, as he entered his office and sat down. "You're right, it was all Max's fault."

"Yep. That's right, all his-he will pay," the man said. "And get your ass out of that chair, I did not say that you could sit down."

"Wh-wh?"

"David, remember I am the wind, you can't hide from me."

David got out of his chair. "Why do you want me here?"

"I don't want you to get hurt," the man answered.

"What?"

"I don't want you to get hurt," the man repeated.

"So, that threat was just hot air?"

"Oh, no," the man said. "This is how you will go but for now you are too important."

The man cleared his throat, "Now David, I have some things for you to do, are you ready to listen?"

David once again held back his fear, "Ok, what is it?"

"Now, before you start, you have to understand that you must do everything exactly as I tell you. Comprende?"

"Comprende," David said.

"Good. The first thing that I want you to do is go to Max's office, and take everything from this case out of his desk and bring it back here."

"What case?"

"What case do you think, you dumb piece of shit?" the man asked. "The Spade case."

"Ok, Ok sorry."

"And keep the cell phone."

David walked over to Max's office and went to his desk, and tried to open the drawer, but couldn't.

"It's locked," David told The Spade.

"There is a hide-a-key under his chair, go get it."

David dropped to his knees and felt around under the chair, already knowing that he would find it. After a few seconds, his hand ran into the small metal box. He put his fingers around it, and pulled it down. He slid open the top, and took out the key. Then he slid it into the slot, turned it, and opened the drawer. Inside, he saw the case file and other places for different folders. He picked it up and walked back to his office.

"Good boy," The Spade said tauntingly. "Now get yours out of your desk." David reached into his top coat pocket, took out his key, unlocked his drawer and took out his copy of the case file.

"Good. Is the most recent murder in there? The scene where you and Max were yesterday; the crime scene where you exploded at the press?"

David was speechless.

"I'll take that as a yes," he said. "Now, I want you to bind both yours and Max's folders together using a rubber band, you have some in the top drawer of your desk."

David had trouble getting the rubber band around the folders because his hands were shaking so hard.

"Oh David, you are doing so good," The Spade said laughing.

"Now look out your window." David did. "Do you see a big plastic bag?"

David said nothing.

"You can just nod."

He did.

"Ok, now put the case files in the bag, I will pick them up later."

"How do I?"

"Just climb out the window."

David opened his window, and crawled out. After he put the case files into the bag, he started to go back in.

"Put it under the bush."

David did as he was told, and then crawled back into his office.

"Very good David. There is one more thing that I want you to do."

"What?" David said.

"I want you go to Eddie's lab." The Spade told him. "And leave your window open."

"Ok," David said, as he made his way to Eddie's lab.

"Keep the cell phone."

David did as he walked into Eddie's lab.

Eddie looked up from his computer. "Hi David, Larry told me you were dropping by."

"Now," David heard the Spade say in a whisper. "DUCK!"

David dropped to the ground and covered his head.

"Hey, David, what's wr..." Eddie stopped

as the knife entered his chest. He fell to the
ground beside David. David felt Eddie's hand
grab his shoulder just for a moment before it
slipped away.

"What did you do?" David asked, horrified.

"I just saved your life," said the Spade
in an angry voice. "You should be grateful."

"But, you just killed Eddie."

"David, David, David," said The Spade in a
disappointed voice. "Have you not learned
anything from this little talk. I am like the
wind. With me, you should always be prepared to
expect the unexpected."

David was too horrified to even realize
that The Spade had hung up.

Part Three: Chief Victor Powell

Since you would save none of me, I
bury some of you.

-John Donne

17

The Set Up

When Chief Powell got home on Friday, he was beat. He had had long weeks before, but none of them had come close to this one.

Like the one where he stayed up for five straight days flipping through web sites and pages trying to find some dirt to crush the old Chief, Saunders his name was. It had taken a while and a lot out of him, but he had finally found something good. Back in eighty-four, Chief Saunders had made a drug bust and five hundred thousand dollars had been collected and checked into evidence. He went back a little further and did a little research on the drug empire that had been taken down. The fortune of the empire was valued at fifty-six million dollars. The house that they raided was thought to have two million dollars in it. Then he went back towards when the bust was made and from the police database found out that four weeks after the bust, Chief Saunders' wife had bought a one point two million dollar house. Chief Powell printed all of these things out, packed them and mailed them to the mayor. Two weeks later he received a letter from the mayor, he was to be awarded for his hard work and dedication to the city. Two weeks after the award ceremony, he was promoted to chief.

One of the other long weeks he had had was in his rookie year back in seventy-six. He was

trying his best to climb the ranks, but he
slowly figured out that he might be stuck at a
desk forever if he did not throw a few punches
below the belt. So he started sneaking around
and listing to other people's conversations and
phone calls, he also dug through the trash cans
trying to find any documents that would end
someone and open a space for him. After a few
weeks he struck gold. He was doing one of his
usual "sneak arounds" when he overheard some
people talking.

  "They'll meet us with the bribe at three
o'clock tomorrow outside the MGM Grand. The
plan is to bump into each other, then we'll
drop our suitcases and switch them."

  "We each get four grams of coke, right?"
the other man said.

  "Four grams each, my man," said the other
again, giving his friend a five.

  After hearing this, Chief Powell snuck off
and told his first Chief, Smith, and let him on
it. Chief Smith liked what he heard and took
Chief Powell out on his first stakeout. They
caught both of the men and the drug dealer, who
swore to God that he would kill the cops for
tricking him, and the little fatty who helped.
After this, he received his first of seven
citations from the mayor. The next week he was
promoted to one of the deputies; and so started
the Chief Powell "ERA".

  Today they had found out that it was him;
he was the one who told the press about the
second Spade. The press had been in the office
all week, as well as his superiors. They were
beyond pissed at him for giving out top secret
information from an ongoing case. He saw no
problem with it. He had heard them talking,
after they thought he left and got some good

information. He had done it before, that was
how he had gained such a good reputation. He
just listened in on others, and told his bosses
or the press before they could. Sure it was
dirty, but you don't make chief by playing
nice. Nice guys always finished last.

Now that this last "eavesdropping" had
come out, the city had launched an
investigation on the entire police force. He
was going to lose everything that he worked so
hard for. So he thought of a plan. He was going
to make up a bullshit story about the CSIs and
the rest of the department and bring them down
too. If he was going down in flames, he was
going to bring as many people into the fire as
he could. All he had to do was make up an
outrageous but believable story and the press
would do the rest, they *always* did. He went
upstairs to change, he was going to go sit in
his whirlpool. Man, he loved it, but he would
lose that too. It always helped him relax, he
always thought better when he was relaxed. When
he was walking back down he caught his
reflection, he didn't remember being that fat.
He needed to lose weight, but that meant
working out, dieting. Way too much work for
him. He could live with being overweight. His
beard was starting to get out of hand too, it
was hard for him to shave with all his flaps of
skin hanging down. When he got to his whirlpool
he hung his towel on the side and went in.
"Aahhhh," he said, sitting down in front of one
of the stronger jets.

The person who had installed it warned him
against having it indoors in a room hardly
bigger then the tub itself. He had told him
off, told him he better do what he is paid to
do or he will get someone else. So the man
left, and it took Chief Powell six months
before he could find someone to install it.

Now what kind of story can I make to take them down with me? he thought.

Maybe I can make up some kind of scandal like that other rookie got fired for.

He sat back and started to think about different things that he could do. He had nothing. He needed to start putting that brain of his to work if he wanted to bring them down too. After about an hour he passed out. The sound of someone furiously banging on the door woke him up.

"God 'nam it."

He got up and saw that the bottom half of his body was pink.

"God 'nam it," he said again.

He put on his towel and walked upstairs. He was too pissed at himself to even notice the hole dug in his basement floor. When he got to the door no one was there. "God 'nam kids." he said as he walked upstairs.

In the shower his beard got in the way quite a bit, so he decided to shave it. He was as careful as he could but he still cut himself numerous times. When he got out of the shower the rash had faded a little. He dried himself off, put little balls of toilet paper over the cuts and went downstairs. He was in the kitchen when he first met him.

"Hey Chief," said a voice from the other room.

He turned around and saw a man in a trench coat and cowboy hat. He was holding a bottle of beer in one of his gloved hands. "How's it going?" he said, raising the other hand in a wave.

"Who de hell r ya?" he demanded.

"Oh, you know who I am," The Spade said to him.

"No, why de hell you in my house?"

"It is your time."

"Time for 'hat?"

"To die."

"'hat!?" he said, scared and confused.

"Let me explain," The Spade said, finishing off his beer and setting it down. "You have been a dick your whole life, which is why no one likes you and you remain unmarried."

Chief Powell had no clue what was happening.

"I believe you have seen my calling card," he said, handing him a card. The Chief turned it over and looked right at the ace of spades. He looked up, now fully aware.

"Yep," said The Spade as he knocked him out with one blow to the side of the head.

When the Chief woke up he could not move his legs. As his vision came back, he looked down and saw that there was cement up to his knees.

"Help!" he yelled.

"Shut-up, you fat piece of shit," The Spade said, stuffing a towel in the Chief's mouth.

The Chief was helpless, he could only watch as The Spade filled the hole with more and more cement. As he was looking around he realized that he was in his own basement. He was going to die in his own home. Suddenly everything he had done shitty in his life came back to him. All the people he pissed off. All the ones he had stepped on. How long would it take for someone to care that he was gone? When the cement got up to his neck The Spade smoothed it out and Chief Powell saw him write something in it. The he got back up and left. The Chief started to panic. He tried too hard to move in the heavy cement and passed out. When he woke up the cement was dry and The Spade was back looking at him.

"It's about time you woke up," he said.

"This is how it is gonna happen."

"In your room there are three wolves, and wolves can smell blood from a good distance away," he said, pulling out a knife. He leaned over the Chief's head, and slashed across his cheek. Blood started to pour out. The Chief screamed in pain.

"Shhhh," The Spade said. "Screaming will only help them find you faster." Then he took off the paper towels and they turned red as blood seeped out, "Just a little something more for your 'friends'."

Then The Spade got up and started towards the stairs. He put his finger on the light switch, "Hope you're not afraid of the dark," he said, as he flipped the switch, and plunged the room into darkness. Chief Powell could hear The Spade walking up the stairs and then out the door. Then he was all alone-all alone with the wolves; all alone with the wolves, in the dark.

18

Race against Time

Max's concussion was not nearly as bad as Larry had made it seem. Though it had been a very hard fall he only had a minor concussion. He was back in two weeks. He had heard about Eddie that night after coming home from the doctor.

When he got to work for the first time since his fall he saw some cars there that he did not recognize. He stood there for a moment, puzzled by these strange new cars. There was a black Sudan and a green compact. He stood there a little longer thinking about it. Then it came to him; they belonged to FBI agents that had come to help with the case, and the person who was taking over for Eddie. They were going to come after David and Max got their little "notes", then after what happened to Eddie they had come straight in. Max hoped that they did not take too much power over the investigation, like they sometimes did. He went straight to David's office and there they were. There were two middle-aged men and one who looked hardly out of college.

"You must me Max," said one of the older men. He had deep wrinkles and bags under his eyes, which were a blazing blue. "Hi," he said, offering his hand. "I am Special Agent Tom Hallaway."

"Nice to meet you," Max said, shaking his hand.

"This man to my left is Special Agent Dominic Lopez."

"Hi," he said, shaking Max's hand. Like Hallaway, the effects of time had started to show on his face as well. His eyes were brown, his hair-line was beginning to recede, and his skin was olive colored "You can call me Dom. if you want to."

"My name is Barry Johnson," said the kid, holding out a shaking hand. His brown hair has slick and parted to the right. His green eyes showed age and wisdom where there was none. "It's a pleasure to meet you."

"What's wrong?" Max said. "I see that your hand is shaking a little."

"Just a little nervous."

"About what?"

"Meeting you, Mr. Levinton. I have looked up to you ever since I studied Orange Creek in school."

"Well, thanks and you can call me Max," Max said, blushing a little. "How long have you worked for the FBI?"

"Oh, he doesn't," Dominic said. "He is one of the greatest young detectives we have ever seen. He is in his second year at the academy and at the top of his class, so we decided to see if his skills would help us on this case."

"Oh," Max said. "What makes you so good?"

"I don't know," Barry said. "Ever since I was a kid, I have been able to notice and figure out things no one else could."

Max looked surprised at the skill level this kid claimed to be at.

He must have seen doubt in Max's eyes. "Tell you what, I will go outside and you take anything from anywhere in this lab, and put it in your office. I bet I can pick it out."

"Alright let's do it."

Barry went outside and Max went searching,

he came back a few minutes later with a book on fingerprinting. He then went to his office and placed it on his book shelf.

Then he went back to David's office and all four of them went to get Barry. He was outside leaning against the building singing to himself.

"We're ready," Max told him.

"Let's do it," Barry replied, following them inside.

"Show me your stuff," Max said, when they got to his office.

Barry walked in and started looking around. He looked on the desk at some pictures, the book shelf, and then went back to Max.

"Well I don't kn..."

Max did not let him finish. "I knew it."

"Let me finish," Barry said, in a content voice. "I don't know how that was supposed to be a challenge. That book on fingerprinting clearly does not belong here."

Max was speechless.

"How did you know that?" David asked.

"Well, first off it does not fit Max's personality. Just look around at his other books: *Inside the Criminal Mind, Tracking Down a Killer, Scene of the Crime.* All his books have to do with finding killers, getting inside their minds and crime scene work. *The History of Fingerprinting* clearly does not belong. Second, it is sticking out further then the other books."

"It, is?" Max said surprised.

"Yep, look it is sticking out about an inch," Barry said, running his hand slowly along the books showing the slight rise and drop when he ran over *The History of Fingerprinting*.

Max walked over amazed, "Wow, you are good."

"And thirdly, it is too new. The rest of these books have slight bends in their jackets, and the top edges are worn out."

No one said anything. Even Special Agents Hallaway and Lopez were shocked by the skill of young Barry Johnson.

"Satisfied?" Barry said.

"Oh, yeah," Max said. "It will be a honor working with such a skilled young man."

This time Barry was the one who blushed, and he cracked a little smile.

At that point Max's cell started to ring.

"Levinton," Max said, when he picked it up.

"Max, glad to talk to you again," said the familiar voice of The Spade.

Max quickly covered the phone, "It's him," Max told the rest.

"Max, there is another victim of mine, and as of now he is still alive, but he won't be for long."

Max waved the rest in to listen.

"So this time if he dies, it will be on you guys."

"Where is he?" Max said. Then he held the phone out a little so the rest could hear.

"You can find him by playing a little game."

"Ok, what is it?"

"You will follow my clues and hopefully make it there in time."

"Where first?"

"The phone at the receptionists deck in one minute, go."

The line went dead and Max and the others ran to the front. Just as they got there they heard a phone ringing. The receptionist started to answer it.

"No," Max yelled." It's for me."

Max leaned over and picked it up.

"What?"

"Water works, fifteen minutes, leave David."

Again the line went dead.

"David he said you need to stay here, and said the next place to go is waterworks."

"It's the Bellagio," David said. "They do water shows all the time."

"Thanks," Max said, as he Hallaway, Lopez, and Barry ran out.

Max and Barry made it easily but Hallaway and Lopez were out of breath. After about twenty seconds, a phone ten yards down started to ring. Max got to it first. "What?"

"The king of the jungle in twenty, leave the Mexican FBI."

"You need to stay behind this time." Max said, looking at Dominic.

"Good." Dominic said. "The next show is about to start."

"Where next, Max?" Barry said.

"He said the king of the jungle. Does that ring any bells?"

Barry thought about it for a second then snapped his fingers. "It's the MGM Grand. Their symbol is a lion, the king of the jungle."

"Man, am I glad you're here," Max said, as they started off again.

When they got to the MGM they had about five minutes to spare. When the phone did ring, Hallaway answered it.

"What next?"

"You see me in the desert, but I am never there, ten minutes. This time you stay, FBI."

Hallaway hung up. "He said that you can see him in the desert, but he is never there, and I need to stay this time."

"He is in the desert but is never there. What does that mean?" Barry said.

Max looked up from a deep thought "He's a

Mirage. You see him in the desert but he is never there. That's where the next place is."

"Well, you better hurry up you only have ten minutes to get there." Hallaway said.

Max and Barry ran off toward the Mirage, while Hallaway went back to the crime lab. This time they got there with a little less time. When they got there they could hear a phone ringing in the distance. They sped up as the pay phones came into view. Max saw someone looking around seeing if anyone was going to answer the phone. The man got up and reached towards it.

As he picked it up and raised it to his ear Max yelled out. "L.V.P.D!! Drop the phone!!"

The man dropped the phone and put his hands up. Max went to explain the whole thing to him, while Barry bent down and picked up the phone.

"Hello?"

"Green Garden Road. The sixth house on your left. Get there as fast as you can, and remember you know about this one so if he dies, it will be on you Barry. Leave Max behind."

Barry hung up and turned to Max "He told me where the next person is. He wants me to go alone."

"Shit," Max said. "I should not do this but..." Max looked around. "I think I can get off the hook." Max said, handing over his gun. "Be careful kid." Barry gave a quick nod of thanks; made sure the safety was on and ran toward the house.

When Barry got to the house he looked around a little to make sure there was nothing set up, then he knocked down the door, and went in. As he was walking around he heard soft growls coming from the basement. He walked over and saw a light switch. He flipped it, and saw two wolves looking at him. He pulled out Max's gun as the wolves bared their teeth, which were covered in blood. He turned off the safety, when they ran for him. He shot off two quick shots. Each one hit a wolf in the middle of the forehead. They fell into a lump halfway up the stairs. Barry saw blood seeping out of the dime holes in their heads, and he saw their brains near the bottom. He breathed a sigh of relief, but did not put the gun away yet. He walked down and saw something that made him want to puke. There was part of a neck sticking up from some cement, there was still blood dripping down. He was too late. He was just a little too late, and now this man had died, because of him. He could have saved him but he was too late. Barry ran back outside as the urge to puke came on stronger. He went into the street and threw up more then he had ever remembered. He went back and sat on the front steps, and tried to fight back tears. It was his fault, all his fault. He had let a man die today. He took out his phone and called Hallaway.

"Hallaway," he answered.

"Hey, can you give the phone to Max if he is around?"

"Yeah sure."

"Hello?"

"Max," Barry said. "He's dead, I didn't make it here in time."

"Oh, shit," Max said. "Barry, I am sorry. Are you sure he is dead?"

"Oh, yeah," Barry said. "His head is gone."

"Gone?"

"Yes, the body is in the basement up to what is left of his neck in cement. There were wolves down there. I am pretty sure that they ate him alive, it was dark. Max, it was dark. How long did he sit there in the dark waiting for them."

Max winced "I don't know. "How bad does it look?"

"Really bad. I had to leave the house so I would not throw up in there."

"God," Max said. "Well where are you? We are coming to the scene."

Barry gave them the directions and was about to hang up when Max spoke again, "Barry, it is not your fault, you could not have stopped the wolves. He was probably dead when you left the MGM."

"Thanks Max, that makes me feel a little better. It was just that neck sticking up from the cement."

"Don't worry, we will be there soon."

"Ok, see you soon Max."

"Bye Barry."

"Bye."

Then he hung up the phone, and Barry waited.

19

A Chip and Chisel

Max, David, Hallaway, and Lopez got there about fifteen minutes later. Barry was still in a sort of daze.

"Barry, are you OK?" Max asked as they approached the house and Hallaway helped David put out the yellow CRIME SCENE tape.

"Yeah, it's just," he said. "I've never seen anything as cruel as that. I mean, he was up to his neck in cement, so he could not do anything to even try to protect himself."

"Well, no offence to you, but there has been and will be a lot, I mean a lot, more cases that you will run into that are worse then this, so you might need to get used to it," Max said, patting Barry on the back.

"Thanks man," Barry said. "What's the bag for?"

Max looked at him surprised. Barry pointed towards the black handle poking out of the bed of Max's truck.

"What makes you think that that's a gym bag? Some of our tool kits have black handles."

"I know that, but not that thin and they aren't made of the same material. So again, what's the bag for?"

"You said that the victim was in cement, right?" Max said, going back to the truck and grabbing the bag, and throwing it to Barry. It did not look heavy to him but looks can be deceiving and this was no exception. When Barry put his hands out to catch the bag it dropped right through his hands. Barry picked it up and looked at Max, blushing.

"Don't worry about it the speed of the throw made it a little heavier. Go ahead look inside."

Barry put it down on the curb and unzipped it. Inside he saw multiple hammers, chisels and metal stakes, "We're going to dig him out by hand?"

"Bingo," Max said. "Jackhammers rattle it too much and can damage evidence. Not all crime work is fun, kid." Max walked over, re-zipped the bag, picked it up and walked in after David, Hallaway and Lopez with Barry trailing at his feet.

"Alright," Hallaway said, looking around. "Where is the body?"

"Right down here sir." Barry said, walking towards the basement.

"You don't have to call me sir, Barry," Agent Hallaway said.

"Sorry sir, it is just the way I was raised."

As they walked down the stairs they saw the dead wolves.

"Damn," said Agent Lopez, first looking at the wolves and then the blood spatter. "You got them son-ova-bitches good, and they were a moving target." The rest looked just as impressed.

"Man, PETA is going to be all over you for this," David said. "But no one else will take a second glace, it was self-defense."

When they got to the bottom of the stairs and saw the neck sticking up from the ground, no one said a word. Max took out his Vic's and after he applied it to his upper lip, he offered it to the others.

"I'll take some of that," said Hallaway.

"Me too," Dominic said.

"What's it for?" Barry asked.

"Vick's has such a strong smell it completely blocks out the scent of a dead body," Max explained. "I would not have made it as a CSI without it."

"Yes, I would love some of that," Barry said, putting some on his upper lip.

When they got to the body Max was the first to see the note written in cement. He quickly pointed it out to the rest.

I write to you from number eight
A man who everyone loved to hate
The final battle does come near
Where one of your blood I will smear
The end will come in autumn
When I will take my final victim

"Holy shit," Hallaway said. "What the hell is this guy?"

"Yeah," David said. "I told you we were going to need some help."

As he snapped pictures of the body and note from multiple different angles, he spoke, "Let's get started on getting the body out the best that we can."

Then they started to chip away the cement. Little by little the cement went further and further down. After the cement had gone down about five inches Barry said, "I got something." They all went over to see. "Look, it looks like a suitcase."

"What the hell is that?" Max said.

"I don't know."

About two hours later they had gotten the cement down far enough to remove the suitcase. Barry reached down and tried to pull it out, it did not budge. Dominic shoved his chisel under the suitcase and moved it around a few times. "Try it now."

Barry pulled and this time it came out with ease. He looked at it "Damn."

"What?" Max said.

"It's got a lock."

"I can fix that," Max said.

Barry handed him the suitcase. Max set it down and hit each clamp with the hammer. They both popped open. "There you go."

"Uh...thanks," Barry said, opening it up.

Barry took one look in, screamed and threw it away.

"What?" David said.

Barry just sat there.

Max went over to pick it up and he too gasped. David, Hallaway, and Dominic walked over. Everyone was speechless. In the suitcase were files for Barry, Hallaway, and Dominic. It had their date of birth, the hospital they were born in, the state. It had all of their schooling from kindergarten to graduate school, and even pre-school for Barry. Max removed the files and there were also pictures of all of them. Under that there was another note.

I know who you are you can't fool me
You are FBI and a detective prodigy
You came from New York, Dallas, and L.A.
Your reasons for coming here I do not know
Maybe those L.V.P.Ds can't handle a little action
I hope you will leave before it's too late
I will show no mercy even on the kid

No one spoke for quite a long time. The phone ringing upstairs broke the silence. They all ran up to answer it. David reached out and pushed out the speaker phone button.

"Hello?" Barry said.

"I trust you got my notes?"

No one spoke.

"All I need is a nod."
They did.
"Welcome to my world of fear."
Then he hung up.

20

Evidence

When the initial shock wore off, they stood silent for a few moments before talking.

"I think this guy must have some kind of mob connection," Hallaway said. "How else could he know everything about us?"

"Or," Barry said. "He is someone on the inside."

"I think the mob connection is more plausible." Max said.

"I think he is bluffing," Dominic said. "He can't see us right now."

"Damn dude, don't say that, you're just egging him on," David said. "I've seen what this guy can do."

The phone rang again.

Barry answered the phone, and after a moment handed it to Dominic.

"Hello?"

"You want to say that again, Wet-back?"

"Excuse me?" Dominic said, in a voice that was too big for his shoes.

"I said, do you want to say that again Wet-back."

Dominic remembered what he said, and because he had been insulted he continued his ego trip, "I think you are bluffing."

"Is this a bluff?" As the man finished, a red dot appeared on each of the detectives, "Take it back or I...I mean we will pull the trigger."

Dominic could not speak.

"All I need is a nod."

They all nodded.

"Good," the dots disappeared. "Be good, and remember, I am always watching." Then he hung up again.

After thirty-five years, Special Agent Domenic Lopez had reached his breaking point, "Oh, damn, fuck this, I can't take this shit anymore." Dominic said, going towards the door.

"Wait," David said. "Let's finish this scene, then if you still want to leave, be my guest."

"Ok," Dominic said. "Alright, I can do that."

Then, with Max leading, they all went back to the basement. When they got back down they grabbed their tools and started to chip away at the cement again, they didn't get too far when they had to leave for the night. They packed up, and went home.

When they all returned the next morning to finish the job, Dominic was not there.

"Damnit," Hallaway said. "He bailed out on us."

"Don't worry," Max said, "We can work today without him, then we'll go talk to him tonight." The rest just shrugged, and they got to work.

After about five minutes, Max yelled "I got something."

They all went over to see what it was. Max was bent down with a pair of tweezers.

"What did you find?" Barry asked.

"I got some hair," Max said, coming up with a small bit of stone in the tweezers. "Got some more blonde hair David," Max bagged it, tagged it, and went back to work. Not much happened over the next few hours before they took their lunch break. Right though as they were about to leave, David found something.

They all went over to see. David pointed
to some gold sticking out from the cement. They
all gathered around and started chipping around
trying to see what it was. After a half hour
they exposed some letters. LVDP.

"Damn," Barry said "it's a cop."

"Yeah, but who?" Max said.

They chipped away some more, and they
exposed the rest of the badge, as well as the
bottom of an ID. When they saw this they
started to work more franticly. After the next
few minutes, they were able to take out the ID.
The case it was in was covered in cement so Max
got some tweezers as pulled it out from the
side. When it was out he gasped.

"Who is it?" David asked.

"It's the chief of police," Max said,
turning it to them. "Chief Victor Powell."

They went to McDonalds for lunch; they sat
at a back table, and talked low.

"Ok," Hallaway said. "So let me see if I
have this so far, first the killer kills your
brother and future sister-in-law," he said
pointing at David. "Then he tries to kill you,"
he said, pointing at Max. "Then he kills again,
but we still don't know who they are yet,
right?"

"Yeah, but we are working on putting their
faces on the news to try to get an
identification."

"Alright," Hallaway said. "Then he blows
up Andy and Ken, and you two get little
'notes'. Then Eddie is killed, and finally with
the killing of the Chief it lands us with a big
zero."

"Yep," David said. "We have nothing on
this guy, guys we think."

"So the hair..." Barry said, as some

special sauce from his Big Mac dripped on him. He wiped it up with a napkin. "Sorry, so the hair that you found, Max, is the only thing we have?"

"Well we also have some blonde hair that we found on the last victims," Max said. "There might be some fingerprints on the badge, but considering what has happened so far, don't get your hopes up."

After they finished, they drove back towards the house. When they turned into the neighborhood they saw the smoke. They looked at each other and David drove faster. When they got back to the scene it was blazing. The fire was everywhere. They watched helpless as the windows began to explode. When the fire truck finally put out the fire half the house had burned down. Anything that could have been in the top floors was gone. And to make things worse, they could not go back in because it was a fire hazard.

They could not do a thing, so they packed up and went home. On the way Hallaway called Dominic's hotel room. There was no answer. He tried six more times, nothing. He quickly called Max, David, and Barry. They all met at the MGM, where he, Barry, and Dominic were staying. They went up to his floor and knocked down his door. They rushed in and found nothing. Then David found the note, he read it out loud.

"I am sorry guys, it was too much, I couldn't handle it."

He put it down, Hallaway looked like he was about to cry. Then they heard a soft tapping. Tap, Tap, Tap. It was coming from the bathroom. Tap, Tap, Tap. They all ran in and Hallaway screamed. Dominic was hanging in the bathtub. The noose was attached to a hook that

he must have put in the ceiling himself. They
all stood there stunned, Hallaway couldn't hold
it in anymore and the tears were flowing down
his face, as Dominic's feet continued to bang
against the wall.

Tap, Tap, Tap...

21

A Suspect

They waited outside for about a half an hour until the coroner showed up.

"How long were you two partners?" Barry asked a still teary-eyed Hallaway.

"A-Almost thirty-three years," he said in between gasps. "He was like a brother to me. No, he *was* a brother to me, I would have taken a bullet for him, and he would have done the same."

"Wow, thirty-three years," Max said. "Was he your only partner?"

"Y-Yeah, we met when we were both in out mid-twenties. He was so excited about coming here, it had been years since he had last been here and the whole way up, he was reading a book on hold'em and was playing on the internet." He just sat there, tears still running down his cheeks.

When Larry finally arrived they let him go inside alone. He came and leaned his head out about ten minutes later, "Um...David? Max? Can you two come in here for a minute?"

"Yeah sure," David said, going in with Max trailing behind him.

After they were inside he led them back to the bathroom, "You two have seen your fair share of hangings, right?"

"Yeah, more then I would have liked to have seen," David said.

Me too," Max said.

"Alright," Larry said. "I was wondering..."

"About what?" David asked.

"How many of those hangings have had four vertebrae's in their mid-back shattered?"

"Excuse me?" David said.

"Did you say four of his vertebrae in his back are shattered?" Max said.

"Yes, when I was turning him I felt a gap in his mid-back, where his vertebras should have been, and there is something else you might want to see as well," he said, turning Dominic and lifting his shirt.

In the middle of his back there was a big pink circle with a spade carved in it and an IX carved in the middle of the spade.

"Holy shit," Max said. "It was that damn guy again."

"What is the 'IX'?" David asked.

"I don't know," Larry said. "I was trying to figure out that before I called you in-Max, you got any ideas?" He asked

Max stood there for a moment rubbing his chin. "Nine."

"What?" Larry said.

"Nine, 'IX' is nine in roman numerals," Max said.

"Why would there be a nine in the spade?" David asked.

Again they looked at Max. He was counting on his fingers, finally he held up his fists. "He's the ninth victim," Max said. "Logan and Ann were the first two," he said, putting up two fingers, "then the next people we are still trying to identify were three and four. Andy and Ken were five and six, Eddie was seven, Chief Powell was eight. Finally, Dominic is nine," he said, now holding up nine fingers.

"So, what's the circle from?" David asked.

"First off, there are also some threads in

his watch band that are the same color as the carpet, so he might have been killed in the main room and dragged in here. You should take a sample of the carpet," Larry said. "The circle, I think that the killer was waiting in the room for him, and when his back was turned he slammed him with a sledge hammer, or something similar. It may have paralyzed him, unless one of his ribs got his heart, in which case he died instantly. I think that that is most likely the case here, because no one heard any screams, and his scream would have been mighty loud."

"Could you go tell Hallaway what really happened," Max said. "I am going to get my things and take a look around."
"Sure," David said, as they both went for the door.

Max walked towards the elevator as David sat down by Hallaway. "Barry, go down and help Max," David said. "I need to talk to Hallaway."

"Sure," he said, as he ran down to the elevator, which Max was holding.

"Hallaway?" David said.

"Yeah," he answered, without looking up.

"Max and I were just inside, and Dominic, well, Dominic did not commit suicide, he was murdered."

Hallaway said nothing for a little bit. "You know, if it makes sense it's kind of a relief that he didn't kill himself. Do you get that?"

"Yeah, that does make sense," David said as Max and Barry came back up.

"Sorry you can't come in to this scene, you're emotionally involved," David said, as Max spread some tape across the door.

"Yeah I know that rule," Hallaway said. "I need some rest anyway."

"Alright, be careful man."

Hallaway went to the elevator to go back to his floor and David went back in the room with Max and Barry.

"Did Max let you in on what just happened?" David asked.

"Yeah, Dominic was murdered."

"Alright, I guess we can go ahead and get started then."

David went back in the bathroom with Larry to help him get Dominic down, while Max and Barry looked around the main room. It was not long after when they found the hammer behind the couch.

"David!" Max yelled.

"What?" He yelled back.

"We found the hammer."

"What?" he said, coming back to the main room as Larry wheeled Dominic out. "You actually found something?"

"Yeah," Max said. "This makes me think that he wants to get caught."

"You mean he's tired of this?"

"No," Max said. "I think that this means that he wants to get caught. I think he wants the attention, like the Washington snipers did.

"Let's check for fingerprints," Barry said.

"I guess we could," Max said. "But, I don't think he would slip up twice in one day."

To Max's and everyone else's surprise they did. They found finer prints all over.

"Maybe we can get a suspect now," David said.

"Only time will tell," Max said. "Only time will tell."

The next day when they got to the lab, they found out the good news. The prints had been matched through AFIS. They belonged to a Richard Jacobs. A forty-five year old high

school drop out, with a mile long rap sheet. He
worked in a Walgreen's on the strip. They had
also identified the second two victims as Rob
and Denise Hurd. They got a warrant from the DA
for Richard's arrest. Then they went to their
detective, Sid Smith, so they could make an
arrest. Sid was forty with graying hair and
eyes that made a shiver run down your back.
They drove down to the strip and watched him
for a little before going in.

        Sid went in by himself, while Max, David,
and Barry waited in their car. Sid walked up to
the girl at the register.
        "Excuse me, is Richard Jacobs in today?"
        "Oh, Ricky," she said. "He's right back
there." she pointed to a man restocking the
soda. He was overweight, with messy hair and a
five o'clock shadow. Wire rimmed glasses
magnified his eyes, which showed hate and
anger. He was wearing a dirty white shirt and
torn up blue jeans.
        "Thank you," he said.
        "No problem," she said. "Have a nice day."
        He walked back starting to unholster his
gun. "Richard Jacobs?"
        "What do you want?" he said, turning
around.
        As soon as their eyes met, he dropped the
bottle of Pepsi he was putting on the shelf and
ran the other way.
        "Hey!" Sid yelled "Get back here!" he said
as he chased him.
        "Freeze or I'll shoot!" Sid warned.
        Richard kept going towards the door. Sid
stopped and shot. The bullet hit him in his
upper thigh. Sid saw blood fly out through the
front of his leg. Richard screamed as he went
down. The lady at the front screamed too, and
put her hands in the air.

Sid ran past her "It's OK Miss, I have the situation under control." He flashed her his badge.

Richard was holding his leg and yelling, "Damn it, you son of a bitch, you shot my fucking leg."

Sid walked up and handcuffed him, and made the cuffs extra tight. "And you watch your language in front of the lady."

"Fuck you, pig."

Sid lifted him up, turned him around and punched him in the nose, drawing blood, "You will shut your mouth right now if you know what's good for you," he said. "You understand me?"

Richard groaned, almost out of breath, "Fuck you."

Sid pressed his gun to the back of Richards head, "I should kill you right now. No one think twice, you a serial murder and me a model representation of the city. You want to take your chances?"

Richard shook his head.

"Richard Jacobs," Sid said, "you are under arrest for the murder of Logan Walker and Ann Neff, Rob and Denise Hurd, Andy Shepherd, Ken Walton, Eddie Jackson, Victor Powell, Dominic Lopez, and for the attempted murder of Max Levinton," he said, and lifted him back up and led him out. "You have the right to remain silent, if you choose to give up that right, anything you say can and will be used against you in a court of law. You have the right to an attorney, if you cannot afford an attorney, one will be appointed to you at no cost. Do you understand these rights?"

"Yeah," Ricky said with a grunt. "This aint the first time I been arrested."

22

The Interrogation

David, Max, and Barry watched from their car as Richard went down, and Sid arrested him. Max was the first to notice the blood spreading around Richard's pants. He leaned over and called for medical assistance. Sid sat Richard down and they watched him get chewed out. Richard did not even flinch, he had been through this kind of thing before. He kept that same "I don't give a shit about nothing" look, while the blood from his shirt soaked his shirt.

The ambulance arrived fifteen minutes later. They first removed the bullet from the leg, then they disinfected the area, and finally wrapped it up. Next they fixed his nose from his "fall". Then Sid shoved him into the backseat of his car and they drove back to the station.

When they to the station they parked in front next to Sid, who was just as rough getting Richard out of the car and practically dragged him in, and walked in. They waited in the lobby while they got set up. Five minutes later, Sid came back, "Alright guys, he is waiting for you in interrogation room B."

"Thanks," Max said, as they walked towards the room. When they got there they all went in.

Richard was sitting at the table with that same 'I don't give a shit about nothing' look. They all sat down around the table. Max placed some pictures of Dominic and Chief Powell around him.

"I have never seen them in my life," Richard said, looking at the pictures at the crime scene.

"Oh really," David said. "Then how come we found this at the crime scene?" He showed Richard the picture of the sledge hammer. "With *your* prints on it."

"I don't know," he said. "Maybe someone stole them."

"Someone *stole* them?" Max said. "Do you know what the chances are that they could steal every one of your prints and then arrange them in a perfect grip and keep them whole?"

"Don't know," he said. "Pretty good I think."

"More like one hundred and sixty billion to one," Barry told him. "You have a better chance of winning the lottery."

"Yay for me," he said. "I gonna win the lottery."

"What is your problem?" David said. "Do you have any remorse at all about what you did?"

Richard leaned forward, "I aint saying anything else till my lawyer gets here."

"Just answer the question," David repeated.

"I don't have to do nothing." Richard said. "I know my rights, I want my lawyer.

"Fine," Max said. "We can wait, we got all day." Then they walked out and waited for Richard's lawyer to arrive.

They waited about forty minutes for Richard's lawyer to show up. They were just about to give up and call in someone else, when he finally came.

"Hi," he said as he walked up. The lawyer looked like he was in his mid-thirties. He had red hair, and a squeaky voice, "My name is Kyle Catford." He peeked in the window. "Is that my client?."

"Yes that is Mr. Jacobs," David said. "Have you been filled in on what he is being accused of?"

"Oh yeah," he said. "I heard attempted murder."

"No, that's just the *little* part," Max said.

"What do you mean the *little* part?" he asked.

"There was one count of attempted murder," David said. "On Max over there," he pointed to Max.

"And the other?"

Max sighed. "He is also under arrest for nine counts *of* murder."

"What," Allen said, beyond shock "Nine counts *of* murder? I've never handled a client like this. He is chained to the table, right?"

"Yep," Barry said. "Go ahead in he won't talk to us."

When they finally got him talking again, it didn't go any smoother now that he had a lawyer. Everything they asked him he answered with a, "You don't have to answer that," or "You can't talk that way to my client." They weren't getting anything.

Finally, seeing that things weren't going so well, Sid came in to help out, "Look," he said to Allen. "You can't just keep your client from talking, we have physical evidence linking him to the crime scene," he pushed forward the pictures of Dominic again. "His prints were found on the murder weapon."

"My client is not saying a word," Allen said.

"That's ok," Sid said, getting up. "We

have all day."

They left with Sid, and started plan B.

"Hope he doesn't mind that the air broke,"
Sid said as he turned the heat all the way up."

They went back in the room, "You want to
tell us what you know?" Sid asked again.

Richard did not even flinch.

"Alright," Sid left and came back with
four water bottles he handed one to Max, one to
Barry, one to David, and kept one for himself.

Little beads of sweat were starting to
form on Richard's forehead.

Max took a big slug of his. "Oh, this
water is *so* cold. It feels *so* good in a hot
room like this."

"I don't think that I can drink much more
of this." David said, acting like he was about
to throw it away. "But, I will," and he took
another gulp.

Sweat was now starting to soak up
Richard's shirt, "If I tell you what I know,
can I have some water?"

Sid took another huge sip, "Yes," he said,
taking another bottle from behind his back and
throwing it to Richard.

He drank about half of it before talking,
"They paid me to whack the Mexican."

"Whoa," Max said. "Who paid you?"

"I don't know, I never saw their faces,
they just gave me the money and I did my job.
This is the first one that I actually killed;
they did the rest of um."

"Wait," David said. "There *are* two of
them." He turned to Max. "That supports our
theory." He turned back to Sid. "What did their
clothes look like?"

"It looked like they were from a western
or something. They had on boots, black gloves,
trench coats, cowboy hats, and a bandana over
their mouths. I saw them at a Halloween party.

But, there was one thing they had on that didn't fit. They had on mirror sunglasses."

"Ok," Sid said. "This is a start."

"When did you first meet them?" Sid continued.

"At work one day. They came in and bought three decks of cards."

David took Max over to the corner. "Three- that means that there is at least one more victim, assuming that they haven't bought any more."

Max and Barry looked at David like he was an idiot and David's face blushed as he realized what he had said.

They walked back. "You said they paid you to do it?" Max asked.

"Yep, I got an extra twenty for the Mexican."

"An extra twenty?" Sid said. "What did you usually do?"

"They paid me to spy on them," he said. "It was weird that they didn't just hire a private investigator for how much they were paying me."

"How much did you get?" Sid asked.

"Ten thousand per person," he said. "In cash."

"You didn't notice anything wrong with them having twenty thousand up front for you?" Sid asked.

"Hey, that's as much as I make in six months. I didn't ask a thing."

"What did you do when you realized that the people you were spying on for them started to die?" Sid asked.

"Well the thing about that..."

"Stop right now, Richard," Allen advised.

"No," Richard said. "I want to clear my name; I don't want to go to death row."

"Well, it might already be too late for

that," Sid said. "You murdered an FBI agent, but," he said. "If you can help us catch these other people, I might be able to pull a few strings and get you life in prison."

"Alright, that's better than waiting on death row," he said. "Now as I was trying to say earlier, I did start to wonder when they started dying. I was gonna call you, I swear but..."

"What?" Sid said.

"When I saw the first news report they called me and said that they would destroy me and everyone that I had ever loved if I told the cops. But I don't think they can hear me in here."

"Yeah," Max reassured him. "Nothing you say will hurt you, we can protect you."

"So they used the scare tactic on you too." Barry added.

"What?" Richard asked.

"It looks like they paid you to spy on them so they would know everything about them. So they could enforce their point better."

"Oh," Richard said. "That makes sense."

"So that was *you* spying on me at the crime lab?" David asked.

"What crime lab?"

"You mean it wasn't you?" David asked.

Before Richard could answer again his lawyer stood up, "That's it," Allen said. "You're not going to listen to me, then I am leaving." He picked up his briefcase and left.

"You do know that you can stop talking at any time now that your lawyer has left," Sid said.

"Yeah, I know, I want to finish.

"No, mister, that was not me spying on you at the crime lab,"

"So how did they get in?" David asked.

"They must have had someone on the inside.

Think about it. How was the person able to get in and out with out any questions? He *or* She must have some kind of connection in law enforcement."

"Great," Barry said. "That only narrows it down to a few thousand in state, and who knows how many more if the killer is from out of state."

"No, he must be in state probably even Clarke county considering that he has such a knowledge of locations."

"Is there anything else you would like to share with us, Mr. Jacobs?" Sid asked.

"No, that's all that I know." He put his hand over his heart. "I swear."

"Alright," Sid said. "Just tell one of the guards if you remember anything else."

"I will," Richard said.

"Alright," He turned to the security guard in the corner of the room. "Take him away."

Max, David, and Barry were walking out when they heard screams. They turned around to see Richard struggling and banging his head against the wall.

"Sedate him!" they heard Sid scream.

They watched as a shot went into Richard's arm. He was still flailing around trying to kill himself, when the tranquillizer started working. He dropped like a sack of bricks, and they dragged him away.

They heard Sid talking in the distance again, "Slap a straight jacket on him and put him in solitary confinement, we don't need our only suspect killing himself before we can get any more information out of him."

They were almost back to the crime lab when they started talking again. "Should we tell Hallaway about the suspect?" Barry asked.

"No not yet," David said. "He's not himself right now, I don't want him going down

to the station and doing something to our
suspect or even worse, killing our suspect,
that would not be good for us at all."

23

A Little Game of Poker

When Max got home he couldn't sleep, he just lay in bed staring at the ceiling, thinking about what had happened that day. He wondered if David and Barry were having the same problem. As if someone had read his mind Max's cell phone started to ring. Max climbed out of bed trying not to wake his wife, and tiptoed to his dresser to answer his phone. The caller I.D. came up as David's number.

"Hello?"

"Max," David said. "I guess you can't sleep either."

"No," Max said.

"Yeah, neither can Barry," David said. "We were going to meet at the Mirage where Barry is staying, play a little poker, and talk about the case. You want in?"

"Yeah sure, I will be there as soon as I can," Max said.

Max hung up his phone and reclipped it on to his belt. Then he grabbed two hundred dollars, wrote his wife a note telling her where he was, got in his car and drove towards a little game of poker.

When Max got there he found them over by the five dollar slots on the east side of the casino. The table that they were sitting at had

two other people at it, but they were at the
far end and were too busy talking about some
new car they were going to buy when they had
enough to go to the high rollers section. Max
took a seat between them and put down his
money. They were already in the middle of a
hand, so Max had to sit this one out. The only
people still in the hand were Barry and one of
the 'high roller' guys. The guy on the other
end table threw in eight dollars.

"Gonna cost you half your stack to see my
cards," he said.

Barry stared straight forward, not even
blinking. Max was impressed by the poker face
he had. Barry pushed forward all his chips.
"All in," Barry said.

"Alright," the guy said, throwing some
more chips in and flipping his cards. "Flush,
King high," he said.

Barry flipped his cards. "Full house,
threes over sixes."

"Damn," the guy said, as the dealer pushed
the chips towards Barry.

"What's been going on?" Max asked,
throwing in his ante.

"Not much," David replied.

Max took a look at his down cards, he had
a seven-two off suit, the worst hand in poker.
He threw them away before there was even a bet.

"Can I get you boys something?"

Max turned around to see a waitress.

"Yeah, sure," Max said. "Can I get a Bud?"

"Sure," she said. "Anyone else?"

"I'll have a Bud," David said, calling the
bet.

"Make that three," Barry said, flipping
his cards over and revealing three kings.

"Shit," the guy across the table said. He
was now out of chips, he went over to an ATM to
get more money.

"Addict," David whispered.

The waitress had come back with their drinks, each of them threw a ten dollar chip on her tray.

When the next hand started Max got a little luckier, he was dealt two aces. He played it slow and just called the blind.

"Did you figure out anything new about the case?" Max asked. "Like something that he said, that we didn't catch?"

"No," David replied. "But I know he is leaving something out, it just seems too simple that he only 'spied' on them."

"I know," Max said. "It can't be that simple.

The dealer put out the flop: Ace, King, Ace. Max again just called so he wouldn't scare anyone away.

The turn card was another king. The first guy bet and Max just called once more. When it got to one of the 'high-rollers', he raised it. His friend folded, as did David. "Don't want any of that," David said, taking a sip of his Bud.

Max re-raised him. Barry folded. The bet was back to the man.

"You're trying to buy the pot," the man said. "I'm all in."

"Call," Max said instantly.

They both stood up.

"Full house: Kings full of Aces," the man said victoriously.

Max flipped his over. "Four Aces."

Barry whistled.

"Damn," the man said, sitting back down and slamming the table. "Damn, Damn, Damn."

"I got it," Barry announced.

"What?" David asked.

"That thing," Barry replied, lowering his voice. "About the case?"

"Well?" Max said impatiently.

"Remember how he ran in to them at a costume party?"

"Yeah," David said. "So?"

"But he also said that he met them first in the store when they were buying cards."

Son of a bitch," Max said.

"What?" David asked.

"He's seen their faces."

After the hand ended they cashed in their chips and left for the department.

When they got there they had to wait in the lobby until they tracked down Sid. After almost thirty minutes, they finally found him; the lady at the front desk told them that he would get there in about twenty minutes. They sat down and said nothing, just waited in the silence for Sid to show up.

"Hey," he said with a yawn as he walked in. "What's the rush on talking to Richard Jacobs again?"

"He's lying to us," David said.

"Excuse me," Sid said. "How do you know this?"

"He's seen their faces," Max told him.

"Again, how did you come across this information?"

"He first met them when they were buying some cards remember?" Barry asked.

"Yeah," Sid said, starting to get irritated.

"He never said anything about them wearing the cowboy costumes when they were buying the cards, he said he ran into them at a costume *party* where they were in the cowboy costumes." He continued.

"My God," Sid said. "Where did you *find* this kid? He is awesome."

"Thanks sir." Barry said, still unable to hold back a blush.

"I think that Mr. Jacobs is going to have an early wake up call."

Max, David, and Barry were waiting in interrogation room C drinking some coffee when Richard Jacobs was brought in, still half asleep.

"What do you want?" Richard demanded. "I was having a nice dream."

"Well sorry about that," Max said. "You can get back to that as soon as you start telling us the truth."

"I have been telling you the truth," he said.

"Stop lying to us," Sid said. "We know you know what their faces look like."

"What?" Richard said confused. "No I don't."

"Yeah, you do." Sid said. "You told us that the first time you met them was when they were buying cards. Then you said that you ran into them again at a costume party. At which they were wearing their cowboy outfits."

The look on Richard's face melted. "Well, you see the thing about that is..."

"I don't care what the reason is, just come clean and tell us what you know."

"Alright," he said. "They looked homeless when they came in, you know all dirty, raggedy clothes, beard crusted in dirt, all smelly. I was gonna tell them to leave, because we've had trouble with the homeless before."

"Yeah, get to the point," Sid said.

"Well, I was going back there to tell them that they needed to leave. When I got back there they were waiting for me like they knew that I would be coming back. One of them looked straight at me and said, 'You want to make some extra money?' At this point I was curious as to what they meant, so I asked him 'How much?' He talked a little with his buddy and said 'Ten thousand per person'. This seemed a little weird to me so I asked them what for? 'We need to find out about the private lives of a few friends.' I saw no problem with that so I asked them when I would get the money and who were the people. 'Come with us, we can give you five thousand up front and give you the list.' So I went up front, and clocked out, I was already working overtime, and I followed them out. They led me down the strip to the MGM Grand. They were on the third or forth floor I think. They led me to a room at the end of one of the halls, on the right side I think. When they let me in I was almost blinded by the reflection."

"What was it from?" Sid said.

"I was wondering the same thing at first and when I got in I thought I was gonna die."

"Why?" Max asked.

"The walls were covered in knives. Every wall, there must have been at least fifty. I could see my reflection in all of the blades. And there was something else too, it stood out."

"What was it?" Barry asked.

"There were pictures of all these different couples and road maps, like the kind you can get from Expedia. Most of the pictures had big red X's on them, and some had green check marks."

"So they already knew who they were going to kill," David said. "Those bastards, they knew even before they got you," he pointed at Richard. "Everything was planned from the get-go," David said. "For how much I hate them, they are pretty damn smart."

"So after I saw the knives, I was gonna run out, but they shut the door on me. 'I thought you wanted some extra money,' one of them mocked. I was so scared I could not even

move. I...I actually wet my pants; I didn't
think that it was true that your bladder let go
when you got scared. That made them even
madder. 'Damn monkey boy, I thought you were a
man, but you wet you pants like a little baby,'
then he held a knife up to my throat. 'You want
to clean that up you little shit, or should I
add a little of your blood to the mix.' I was
crying by this point because I didn't want to
die. I bent down and wiped up the pee with my
own shirt. When I got back up they put the
knife in my hand and made me squeeze. Then they
took it out. 'Now we have your prints, monkey
boy, you're stuck doing this job now.' So I sat
down and listened to their instructions. 'First
of all, you need to track them down in the
order that they are now, it is extremely
important that we have them in the right order.
As soon as you get everything there is to know
about them, come straight back here and you
will get the money. Then as soon as you see
their names again, start working on the next
ones and so on, got it, monkey boy?' I nodded.
'Good,' he said, as his friend led me out. 'And
remember, monkey boy, we have our eyes on you.'
Then they pushed me out and threw my piss
soaked shirt at me. 'Don't be late.' Then they
closed the door."

      "So when you ran into them at the
Halloween party they gave you the list?" Sid
said.

      "Yes," Richard said. "That's when I
started."

      "Alright," Sid said. "you can go back to
bed now."

      "So you know what we have to do now,
don't you," Sid said, as they walked out.

      "Yeah," Barry said, with a little fear in
his voice. "We have to go to the house of

knives."

24

Trust No One

It did not take long for them to get a warrant to gain entry to the room they needed in the MGM Grand, as the evidence was overwhelming. As soon as the D.A.'s office opened for the day they went in and got the warrant.

When they got there the manager was not too happy with the warrant, and the fact that they didn't know exactly which room, or even floor.

Since the third floor was the closest, they checked there first. Max and Barry went to the left halls with one of the bellboys, and David and Sid went with the manager to the right side of the halls. All the doors on the left side at the end of the hall did not have anything out of the ordinary in them. They got back to the center of the floor about the same time that David, Sid, and the manager did.

When they got to the forth floor, they again split up and went to separate sides of the floor. This time they got a little luckier. The first room that Max and Barry opened was the house of knives, just like Richard had described it.

When the door first opened light shone on to them, forcing them to shut their eyes. They closed the door and Max called David, telling them that they had the room. When they got there, Sid unholstered his gun, and went in first. He was lucky that there was no one in the room because like Barry and Max, the shine from the blades made him duck down as he went in. After about five minutes they heard Sid call from inside the room, "Clear!"

They all walked in, covering their eyes. When they were finally in the room, they were all speechless. All of the walls were covered in knives, just as Richard had said. The knives were all different sizes. Some were small little daggers; some were normal size knives like the kind that had been used so far. There were also some butcher knives, and even a few machetes.

"Oh my God," David said. "I thought Richard was exaggerating when he said that the walls were covered in knives, but he was right."

They continued walking around examining the knives and taking pictures. In all there were seventy-two knives hanging on the wall; then they found the pictures.

It was an accident really; David lost his balance when he tripped on his shoelace. He fell forward, grabbing onto a knife handle for support, surprisingly it held him up. Puzzled, he took it off the wall when he had regained his balance; he heard a low buzzing sound like a motor. The rest heard it too and they all gathered around as part of the wall came down revealing a wall of pictures.

They were of the victims at work, home, in the street going into their house. There were also notes tacked to the pictures. Over most of them, like Logan and Ann, Rob and Denise, Chief Victor Powell, there big red X's with an Ace of Spades tacked in the middle. There was one more, without notes, and with out X's.

"Looks like there is one that they didn't get to yet," Sid said. "Who are they?"

"I don't know, the map is gone," Max said. "Is there any way that we can find out who they are?"

"I have an idea," Sid said. "it's kind of dirty though."

"What is it?" David asked.

"We could," he said snickering, "we could put up a warrant for their arrest, and put it on the news."

"What?" Max said. "That's not kind of dirty, that's really dirty-but kind of smart."

"Let's do it," David. "I think we can explain it to the D.A."

"Absolutely not," the D.A. said, later. He was a veteran of the law, almost eighty. "That is crude, that is unfair to them, and that might even be unconstitutional."

"But, sir..." Sid begged.

"No buts," the D.A. said. "I am not going to give you a warrant and that is final."

Barry grabbed the picture of the couple and shoved it on his desk, "Look here sir," he said. "If you won't give us a warrant, we will not be able to find and protect these people. Then when they die," he pointed at the D.A. right in the face. "It will be on you, try and live with that." Then Barry turned around and walked out.

After Barry had left, the D.A. looked back to Sid, Max, and David, his face now unsure about what to do, "I have been doing this for almost forty years, and I have made many sacrifices, and almost ruined my marriage. Last week my doctor told me that I have prostate cancer and have only a few months left. I have wished many times to take certain actions back, and now I get a chance."

"Are you saying what I think you are saying?" Max asked.

"No," he said.

They sighed.

"But I do have a lunch break in about an hour, and if I happen to leave my door unlocked, there might be a signed warrant that will go missing from my desk."

"Thank you sir," Sid said. "You won't regret it."

"Regret what?" He said smiling.

An hour later they watched as the D.A. walked out of his office, told his secretary to hold his calls for the next hour, and finally walked out the door. Sid carefully snuck into his office, opened the desk drawer and found a blank, already signed, warrant. Then he snuck back out, and made it just in time. As soon as he walked out the Assistant D.A. came down the hall and knocked on the door.

"I think he just went to lunch," Max said.

"Oh," he said turning around. He was much younger, probably in his late thirties. He had brown eyes and blonde hair tied up in a pony tail, "Thanks, I'll check back in about an hour, he usually eats in about an hour."

They all gave a little wave as he left, then they made their way to the news station.

They made it in time for it to be on the twelve o'clock news. They all watched from the crime lab.

When the news started they went over the stories and when it showed the anchors they did their story first.

"Breaking news, the police have two suspects in a recent bank robbery," a picture of the two came up beside her. "If you have any information on the whereabouts of these two, please contact the Las Vegas Crime hot line at 1-800-solveacrime. That's 1-800-solveacrime." She sat up straight, "We now go to Josh for the weather. Josh?"

"Thank you Helen, today..."

Max shut off the TV. That was the only thing that they were interested in.

"All we need to do now is wait for our victims to be turned in." said Sid as they went down by the phones. After about five minutes the first call came in.

"Hello?" the women said said, answering the phone.

"Yeah," said a young woman's voice. "That girl goes to my gym."

"Ok, ma'am," she said handing the note to David, "Do you know her name?"

No," she replied. "But I can tell you that she comes to the gym out on 5th street every weekday from two to three o'clock."

"Ok," the lady said said, writing it down and handing it to David. "Thank you ma'am."

"Glad to help," she replied, hanging up.

"The female victim goes to the gym over on Johnson weekdays from two to three." David read from the note

"Great," Sid said. "That helps us a lot."

Then another one of the phones started to ring, a man beside her answered it.

"Hello?"

"How could you do that?" said an angry male's voice.

"Do what?" He asked.

"Don't play dumb with me," the man said, getting annoyed. "You just put my wife's and my picture on the news and accused us of robbing a bank."

"Wait," he said. "You are the victim?"

"Yeah, you can call it that," he said. "Now why the hell would you put something out like that? My wife is very upset. I should sue you for slander."

"Wait, don't do that sir," The man pleaded said.

"Give me one good reason why I should not." he said angrily.

"Hold on," he handed the phone to Max. "Talk to them."

"Yes sir?" Max answered.

"How could you do such a thing like this?" he asked Max.

"We just saved your life by doing that."

"Really," he said. "And just how did you accomplish that?"

"Have you heard of the serial killer out there right now known as The Spade?"

"Yeah," he said. "It's been all over the news. Why?"
"We recently came across some evidence that led us to the hideout of the killer. In his room there were pictures of all of the victims that he has killed so far."

"So," the man said, getting annoyed. "What's that got to do with me?"

"A picture of you and your wife was next in line," Max said. "If you and your wife don't come down to the station soon, you two will become the tenth and eleventh victims of The Spade."

Ten minutes later they arrived at the station, they were both in their mid-thirties. The woman had shoulder length blonde hair, blue eyes, and not a wrinkle in sight. The man had red hair, which was starting to turn gray, and his face was starting to crack.

"Why us?" the woman asked. "Why does he want to kill us?"

"We are trying to figure that out ourselves," Max said. "As of now, we don't see any pattern in these killings."

"Do you have any suspects yet?"

"We have someone," Max said. "But he is not The Spade, he was the one that led us to

the hideout that led us to help protect you
two."

"Well, I don't know if this is allowed,"
she said. "But could we thank them?"

Max looked at David, David looked at Sid.
"I guess we can do that," he said.

They all walked down to the cell where
they were keeping Richard.

"Sir," she said.

Richard looked up. "What?"

"I would just like to thank you for your
help that led to protecting us from that man."

"You're not safe."

"W-What?" she said.

"No one can protect you from him." He
looked at them "He is smarter then you," he
began to cry. "he is smarter then all of you."

Sid started to lead them away, "Don't
worry about it; we can put you in witness
protection. Get you fake names, fake IDs and a
fake background. You can stay on the down low
until all of this clears up."

"Thank you," the man said.

"Are you sure you can protect us?" his
wife asked. "That man..."

"'That man,' is under arrest for eight
counts of association and one count of murder.
I don't think you should take any threats too
seriously, he's just trying to scare you."

"Alright," she said.

"Now just stay here, until we can get some
things together for you."

"Thank you again," the man said.

"Don't worry about it." Sid replied.

"Look out!" Sid heard Barry yell.
Sid ran back to the cell-Richard had a gun.

"What happened?" Sid asked.

"He said he had something to tell us about
the case, and when I went to listen he pulled
me up against the bars and stole my gun," Max

said.

They all looked at Richard.

He was snickering, "You have no idea how strong they are."

"Wait," Max said. "We can help you."

"No one can, it's too late, no one can stop them."

"Yes," Sid said. "We can, just tell us and we can help you."

"No, you will never understand the madness and perfection of their plan." He put the gun under his chin.

"Don't!" They all yelled.

Richard was laughing now, shaking his head. "You have no idea how far up this goes." Then he pulled the trigger, and their only suspect blew his brains all over the cell.

Part Four:
Walter and Iva

Where there is mystery, it is generally
suspected there must also be evil.
                              -Lord Byron

25

The (Un)protected

It has been four months now since Richard killed himself. It took a week to get the cell cleaned out. Things had cooled down a little bit. The press had not mentioned anything about The Spade, besides the mini-articles near the back of the paper, in almost two months. The last thing that they had reported on was Richard killing himself in custody.

It was never ending for a month straight, they wouldn't leave the station. Everyday as he entered and left he had to fight his way through them, while cameras went off and microphones were being shoved in his face with questions shouted at him. "Mr. Smith, what are you going to do now that Mr. Jacobs has killed himself?", "Mr. Smith, what does this do for the investigation?" and "Mr. Smith, do you have any leads or suspects at this time?" He never even uttered a word, he just kept his head down, and pushed his way through. After a few days, he got tired of it, and started to sneak in and out of the back door when he got there and after the day was over. For a while he got away with it, and no one caught him, until one day.

It started like any other day. Like any high pressured, press swamped day. Everything was going his way, he got the warrants that he needed and he cracked a suspect, one that had robbed three houses. As the day was beginning to draw to a close, he locked up his office and snuck out. When he got to his car he noticed a woman sitting on the hood of his car. She was a fine blonde with intimidating blue eyes. Her breasts were the size of grapefruits.

"May I help you?" he asked her.

"Yeah, at least I think you can," she said.

"Well," he said. "What can I do for you?" he asked as he edged closer.

"I'm a news reporter and I was wondering if there was anything that you could tell me about The Spade case," she said, taking a few buttons off her already nearly see-through shirt, revealing the top of her white cotton bra.

"Well, it all depends," Sid said, getting closer. "What's in it for me?"

"Oh," she said. "Your reward will be very, very nice," she replied, leaning into him as they jumped into the car.

When he took her home he took out the whiskey, they both had a few glasses before they went to the bedroom.

The next day Sid woke up with a major hangover. He could hardly remember anything about the night before. He went to the bathroom and splashed cold water on his face. That woke him up a little, and then he noticed the lipstick on his shirt collar. Things were starting to come back, he remembered taking a lady home. Suddenly he felt the whiskey start to come back up. He dove for the toilet and emptied his stomach. Then he saw the condoms in the trash. *Oh shit, what did I do last night?* he thought. He turned on the shower and let it get cold, which always helped his hangovers. When he got out he felt a little better. He wiped the mist off the mirror and saw the message written in red lipstick.

Sid, thank you for the great time last night and the location of my next victims. I was a little mad when you took them away, but now all is forgiven. Unfortunately for you, this won't stay in Vegas. Ciao!

The bottom was marked by a kiss, surrounded by a spade. *Holy shit!* he thought. *What have I done?*

After his hangover cleared up a little more, he called Max. He picked up after three rings.

"Hello?"

"Max?"

"Yeah," he said. "Wait, this is Sid, isn't it?"

'Yeah, it's me."

"What's up?"

"Well, last night I...um...sorta..."

"What?" Max asked.

"I got drunk with this reporter I met, and things happened and I slipped some information about the whereabouts of the victims that we protected."

"You what?" Max said surprised.

"I know," Sid said. "I must have really gotten drunk last night, or she slipped me something. Whatever it was I cannot remember a thing."

"So how do you know that you slipped some information about the victims?"

"I was trying to remember and so I took a cold shower, that usually helps my hangovers."

"Is this going somewhere?" Max asked, getting a little impatient.

"When I got out of the shower I looked into the mirror to shave and there was a note written in lipstick."

"What did it say?"

"Sid, thank you for the great time last

night, and the location of my next victims. I
was a little mad when you took them away, but
now all is forgiven. Unfortunately for you,
this won't stay in Vegas. Ciao!"

"Damn," Max said. "This is some hard shit,
we have to get out to them pretty soon."

"Yeah," Sid said. "before it's too late."

"Mr. and Mrs. Frank," as they were called
now, were the luckiest people on earth. They
had won a trip to Vegas through an office pool.
Then when they got there, they won a new car
from one of those slots on the strip that you
can play for free. Then on their last pull on
slots, on their last night of their trip, they
won the three million dollar jackpot. So they
decided to buy a yacht, and move to Vegas. Yep,
the Franks were the luckiest people on earth.

"Mrs. Frank" came home from the store at
five o'clock. She purchased all the basic needs
for the upcoming week. She had coffee grounds,
fruit, beer, diet Pepsi, and some meat. She got
a lot of meat; they were going to have a
barbeque. She stepped onto the rocky dock,
care-fully balancing the bags so nothing would
fall. The door slammed open when she got there,
almost knocking her into the water.

"Damn it Walter!" she screamed. "You
almost knocked me into the ocean; do you know
what kind of gross things probably live in
there? I just got my hair done."

"Sorry baby," Walter said, taking the bags
in one hand and putting the other around her
shoulder. "Just trying to help, and remember
its *Ben*."

"Well be more careful next time," she said
kissing him. They went in and began to prep for
the barbeque. Walter began to season the
burgers and steaks, while Iva (Lucy) checked on

the ribs, already soaking in marinade.

She yelled up from the lower floor. "How long have the ribs been soaking?"

"I think about six hours," he yelled back.

"Seems long enough," she said bringing them up. "Let's make the sauce."

The first guest, Robert, showed up at ten to six, after that they just poured in. When everyone was there they went out to the deck and started. Iva sat at one side talking to her friends, while Walter manned the grill and talked to his buddies.

"So Ben," Robert said. "Are you thinking about playing at the World Series of Poker? It's coming up soon."

"I don't know," he said. "I haven't played in a long time."

"Oh don't worry about it," Alex said. "It starts in a few months, and with your luck, you could go far."

"Yeah I might try it out," he said, knowing he couldn't. "The buy-in is ten thousand right?"

"Yep," Robert said. "And you have a chance to turn it into a few million."

"I don't care what the prize is," Walter said, flipping the burgers and turning the hotdogs. "I just want that bracelet." Walter was proud of that comment, made him fit in more. While in reality he could care less about the bracelet-give him the money.

"Oh yeah," Alex said. "The super bowl ring of poker."

"Why don't we play a little after dinner?" Robert suggested.

"Alright," Walter said. "Got a table or something?"

"I got a nice one," Alex said, taking a sip of his Bud. "We can play at my house."

"Great," Walter replied, taking off the

burgers and dogs, and putting on the ribs for a quick smoke for some extra flavor.

"Hundred dollar buy-in sound alright?" Robert asked.

"Sounds fine," Walter agreed.

"Hundred sounds okay to me," Alex said.

The barbeque was a huge success, everyone loved all the food. The last person left at about nine. Iva was sitting by the TV.

"Honey," Walter said. "I am going over to Alex's to play a little poker."

"OK," she said. "If you get back after eleven, be quiet."

"I will," he said, leaning down and kissing her. "Love you."

"Love you too." Then he left.

Alex's poker table really was nice. It had dark green felt with chip and cup holders. The chips were real nice too; eleven point five gram clay chips.

Damn, Walter thought *I wish I could live like this forever; maybe I should start going to the casinos more often so this little fantasy can become a reality.* After about an hour and a half, no one was even focusing on the game. They had gone through about seven or eight beers each. They were just sitting messing around. Walter won the pot with a pair of kings even though Alex had three of a kind, and Robert had a straight, they were all too drunk to play seriously. While he was reaching in to grab the pot he spilled his beer.

"Whoops," Walter said laughing. He picked it upside down. "Whoa," he dropped it on the floor. "I'll get it." He leaned down to pick it up, and when he stood up he hit his head on the bottom of the table, knocking himself out. Alex and Robert collapsed with laughter. They both passed out in their chairs an hour later.

Walter woke up a few hours later. His

vision was still a little fuzzy, and he couldn't move. He could see a woman. He felt ropes around his legs and ropes being tied around his arms. He looked around and could just hardly see a man pulling the ropes tight. He cringed at the pain of the robes. He could feel them starting to cut down into his skin.

"Iva?" he asked confused.

"No sweetie," the woman said.

"Who are you?"

"You don't need to worry about that, it will all be over soon," she said, stroking his hair.

"What will?"

"Don't worry," she said, getting up.

Walter's vision had come back into focus. He could clearly see the woman and the man. They both were dressed as cowboys.

"Iva!" he yelled.

"I'm right here."

He looked to his right and saw her laying beside him, tied up as well. He reached out and grabbed her hand. "What's going on?"

"I don't know," she said in tears. "But I think that it's something bad."

"Shut up you two," the man said angrily.

"Who are you?" Walter said. "What do you want with us?"

"Yeah," Iva said. "What are you doing here?"

"We are here to empty your bodies of your soul," he said. "Your death will be the last in a series of killings that will lead us to our ultimate goal."

"You are part of something bigger than you can ever imagine," the woman said.

"But why us?" Iva asked.

"No particular reason," the man said. "Just the randomness of a complex procedure."

"Just finish it," the woman said, getting

impatient.

The man raised his gun.

Walter and Iva closed their eyes and waited for the blast of the gun. They heard the blast but felt no pain. Three more blasts, still no pain. They opened their eyes and saw four holes in the floor.

"WATER!" they said together.

"Ah, yes," the man said. "The most abundant, strongest thing on earth will force its way through the floor of this overpriced boat, and engulf you with its power."

The man dropped the gun on the floor and left the room with the lady.

"Look," Iva said, motioning to the floor.

Alex strained to look, and he saw water starting to bubble through the bullet holes in the floor. It started to puddle up and stream towards them. It touched Walter's foot; the temperature of the water shocked him. It was colder than ice.

Walter reached his hand up towards his wife, she grabbed it. "I love you, so much," he said. "More than you think, you are the best thing that ever happened to me."

"I know, I can see it in your eyes when you look at me," she said, tears starting to run down her face. "I love you too."

They squeezed each other's hands, and cried.

26

All Washed Up

"This is the place," Sid said as they pulled into the dock.

"Where is the boat?" Barry asked.

"It says here that it is the last boat on the right."

They all ran down towards the edge of the dock. They could hear the drone of the coast guard's helicopter overhead.

Sid led the way as they made their way towards the boat; their footsteps were echoing all around the area. When they got in view of the end of the dock, they slipped in a huge puddle of water on the relatively dry dock. Sid went down first, Max, David, and Barry couldn't slow down in time, and they tripped over him.

"Shit!" Sid yelled struggling to get back up. He fell back down the first time after stepping in some slime. He managed to get back up on his second try. Max and Barry got up as well. David stayed on the ground. Sid and Max started towards the edge of the dock again, while Barry went over to check on David.

"Go," David said, as Barry leaned down to check on him. "It's just a little sprain, I'll be fine."

Barry nodded and ran toward the edge of the dock with Sid and Max. The dock suddenly ended, much like when you reach the deep part of an ocean or lake. The sudden drop took Sid by surprise, he started to fall in but at the last second Barry grabbed his arm and pulled him back up.

"Thanks," Sid said gratefully.

"No problem," Barry replied.

"Where's the boat?" Max asked.

"I don't know," Sid said. "It should be right here."

David limped forward. "He must have taken them somewhere else, so it would be harder to catch his trail."

"Yeah," Sid said. "Of course," he pulled out his radio. "Be on the look out for a..."

Barry put his hand on the radio, "He didn't take them."

Sid put his radio down, "How do you know? I need to get this description out so they can find the boat. Show me some hard proof."

"Look," Barry said, pointing at the post that boats were tied too. Sid put his flashlight over it. There was still a rope attached to it. The rope was going into the water at a forty-five degree angle, "The rope's still attached to the dock, he didn't take them—he sunk them."

"My God," Sid pulled his radio back out. "Forget that last statement, I need a team of divers, repeat I need a team of divers ASAP!" He put it back down, "Let's just hope that we're not too late."

The divers showed up five minutes later. They went down in a group of three. They came back up five minutes later. "We found them," one of the divers said. They went back down with chains to hoist up the boat. They came back up, and gave a thumbs up, as they started to hoist up the boat.

Max, David, Barry and Sid watched with coffee in their hands as they lifted the boat out of the water. The steady drone of the lift was the only sound anyone could hear. When the top of the boat was visible the lift started to stall, "What the hell?" the operator said, pushing buttons and pulling levers trying to get the lift started. The top of the lift, above the pulley, snapped. The houseboat dropped back down, this time the dock could not withstand the weight, and the edge of the dock along with two divers and a cop, sank back to darkness.

After about an hour they finally got the houseboat back up. When the water had been drained, they allowed Max, David, and Barry to go in. Sid waited outside and helped keep watch.

They walked around the dripping houseboat, amazed at the size of the crime. Barry walked into the bedroom and stopped cold.

"Guys," Barry said. "I found the bodies."

Max and David walked in and had the same reaction that Barry did. There were two bodies, one was chained to the bed; the other was tied to the floor with ropes. They were holding hands. They were slightly bloated with rigor mortis just beginning to set in. On the wall behind the bed there was a giant spade burned on to the slightly faded ocean green wall.

Max started to take pictures of the scene, when Larry came in, "Hey guys," he said. "What do we have?"

They just made a little gesturing motion towards the wall.

"Oh," he said with stupidity in his voice after noticing the spade on the wall. "I see that our little friend The Spade left us some more of his handiwork."

"Yeah, we were just waiting for you so we could start processing the scene."

"Alright then," Larry snapped on some latex gloves. "Let's get started." He bent down beside the male's body. "Ok, slight inflammation of the..."

"Max!" Sid yelled from the dock.

Max sighed. "Fill me in later, Sid must have found something important, or he found some people who knew our victims."

Max walked out to the dock where Sid was waiting with a man and a woman in robes. The woman's was pink and fluffy, and the man's was blue with red squares, a bit thinner then his wife's, but still strong enough to keep the cold out.

"These people are Mr. and Mrs.?"

"Kenneth," the man answered, holding out his hand.

"Hi, Mr. and Mrs. Kenneth." he said, shaking his hand and then his wife's.

"You can call me Alex, and this is my wife Margaret." Max could smell beer on his breath.

"Alex," Max said. "How much did you have to drink tonight?"

"Enough to empty three twelve packs with Robert and Ben," his wife chimed in.

"Alright," Sid said, taking that down. "Alex, what is the last thing that you remember about Walter and..." Sid flipped through his notes. "Iva".

"Why are you calling them that?" Margaret asked.

"Those are their real names; they were part of the witness protection program."

"And he still found them?"

"Well yes," Sid said. "We are still trying to figure that out. Can you tell me what you remember about tonight?"

"Well they had a barbeque tonight, great food, they're really good cooks," he said. "Didn't taste too well coming back up though."

"Little too much information," Sid said, continuing taking notes. "What else do you remember?"

"Then I think we played poker for a few hours," he said.

"Yeah," Margaret said. "You kept me up till almost one o'clock."

"When did Walter leave?"

"I don't remember him leaving," Alex said. "The last thing that I remember about tonight was that Ben, I mean Walter, hit his head on the table or something."

Sid looked up from his freshly taken notes, "Then what?"

"Yeah," Alex said nauseously. "Then I..." Alex covered his mouth and ran towards the edge of the dock and emptied his stomach of whatever was left inside.

His wife walked over to him and started rubbing his back. "Are you OK sweetie?"

Alex nodded and slowly stood up. His face was ghostly pale and he was starting to sweat, "I need to go and lie down."

"Wait," Sid said. "What happened after Walter hit his head?"

"I passed out."

"That's all?" Sid asked.

Alex nodded looking like there was something besides beer making him sick, "Yeah, I woke up and noticed that he was gone."

"Thanks," Max said. "This might not seem like much, but this will help us more than you know. It will help us put together a timeline."

Max walked back over to Sid, "I'm not to sure how much of that we can believe," he said. "Let's find this Robert and see what he says."

"Way ahead of you Max," Sid said, pointing to the other edge of the dock. Max could just make out a man coming forward with a cop.

When he got there, Max asked him the same

questions that he asked Alex.

"The last thing that I remember about last night was Ben hitting his head, then I remember Alex shaking me up. I woke up and Ben was gone."

"Alright," Max said finishing the notes. "Thank you for your time, this helped out a lot."

Robert yawned "No problem man, I gota go sleep off this hangover from hell."

"Have a good night sir," Max said.

"You too," Robert said, in the middle of a yawn.

Robert walked back towards his houseboat, as Max walked back over to Sid, "I think we can put it in the record that the last place that Walter was tonight was at Alex's house playing poker and getting drunk."

"Good times," Sid said.

"What?" Max asked surprised.

"Nothing, nothing," Sid said.

"What else do we have on the barbeque that they had tonight?" Max asked.

"Not much else, we have five witnesses that saw Walter, Robert, and Alex leave early. Three that say all three stayed the whole time, and one that said that he saw them leave with Burt Reynolds."

"Really?" Max said. "You check him for drugs."

"Yep," Sid said. "We took a sample of his blood while he was asking me what I thought of the Trojan horse."

"Huh," Max said.

Max went back into the house just as Larry was leaving with the bodies, "Find anything?" Max asked.

"Actually we did," Larry said. "Go ahead back in David and Barry are waiting for you to start processing the rest of the scene."

"Alright," Max said. "Have a good morning, Larry."

"You too, Max." Larry said, as he loaded up the bodies into the van.

Max walked back into the house, and reentered the bedroom. David was taking pictures of the part of the floor where Walter was, and the bed where Iva was.

"What did you guys find?" Max asked.

"We found some fingerprints on the bed posts, and some hair on the ropes," David said.

"How?" Max asked. "The boat was under water, they would have been washed away."

"The fingerprints were taped over."

"What?"

"There was tape, over the print," David repeated.

"So he was trying to save his print."

"Exactly."

"And the hair?" Max asked. "Was that taped too?"

"No," David said. "That was caught in between the rope and the male's arm."

"Walter."

"Huh?"

"His name is Walter, and the woman is Iva."

"Oh ok."

"So, back to the hair," Max said. "Do you think that it was left on purpose too?"

"No," David said. "I don't think that she meant to leave the hair."

"She?" Max said. "How do you know?"

"Long and blonde," David said.

"Is it like the hair we found in Rob and Denise's scene?" Max asked.

"Yeah-as a matter of fact it is." David said thinking about it. "So why did she and possibly he too, leave the fingerprint?"

"I have a good feeling that it is not theirs," Max said. "I think that they are trying to set someone up."

"Yeah," Barry said. "It makes sense that it would not be theirs."

"Why do you think that?" Max asked.

"Well," Barry said. "Up until we got Richard, you two didn't find anything at any of the other scenes. The only time you found good enough evidence to make an arrest was when Richard did it, and he is far less experienced than they are."

"Good point," David said. "So now how are we going to know if the hair was placed as well?"

"Sid," Max said.

"Sid?" David asked. "I don't think that Sid would know if we don't."

"No," Max said. "The whole reason that Walter and Iva were killed was because Sid got drunk, and yapped to a beautiful stranger."

"So," David said. "When we match the hair, if it belongs to the woman that seduced Sid, we got one of our killers."

"Exactly," Max said.

"Unless," Barry said, breaking in. "That whoever killed these people is another person like Richard."

"Let's not think bad thoughts like that." David said.

"Or, this guy or gal *really* is starting to slip up." Barry said.

"Yeah," Max said. "I think that he is doing it on purpose, because in the first scene we found nothing, in the second we found hair. Then in the last scene we found fingerprints of one of the associates."

"But," David said. "Barry did have a good point about Richard not being as good about evidence as them. I mean, he did leave the hammer at the scene."

"Yeah," Max said. "Again, another very good point."

"So why is he doing this on purpose?" Barry said.

"He wants to get caught," Max said. "People like him want attention."

"Max?" David said.

"Yeah."

"Could you cut out the floor surrounding the bullet," David asked. "We might be able to compare bullet holes."

"Sure," Max said, going over to one of the bullet holes and cutting around it, six inches on each side. He picked up the section of the floor he had just cut out and bagged it.

Max then joined Barry and David in processing the scene. It was then when Max noticed the sheet sticking out from the mattress. It was not sticking out very far, it looked like a tag at first sight, and it was the same off-white color as the mattress. Max went over and snapped a picture just in case. Then he took some tweezers and slowly pulled it out. It was folded neatly, a perfect square actually. Max decided that he would open it when he got back to the lab, it was still very wet and he didn't want to risk ruining what could possibly be a very important piece of evidence. Besides, even if it wasn't wet, he didn't have the right tools to open it up.

"What did you find?" David asked.

"I don't know yet," Max said. "It was sticking out of the mattress; I thought it was the tag until I got a little closer."

"Do you think it's another note?" David asked. "They might be leaving us clues, to help get caught faster."

"Like the DC snipers," Barry said.

"Exactly," Max said. "With every note they

leave us, we get closer to finding out who and where they are."

"We should look around more by the mattress, to see if they left us anything else."

So they carefully lifted up the mattress to see if there was anything else under the mattress. And there was. It was another piece of paper folded to a size no bigger then a playing card. Barry did the same thing as Max and then he went back and kept looking. They found three more. One was under the bed post, another was behind a picture of Walter and Iva at their wedding, and the third was under a lamp on a bedside table next to the right side of the bed.

"We should hurry up and get these back to the lab before they dry up and stick together," Max said, as he got his stuff together and began to put his tools and evidence away.

"Well, I guess at this point it's safe to say that they are trying to get caught," David said.

"Yeah," Barry agreed. "I just hope that they don't have any more tricks up their sleeves."

27

C♠r Bomb

Once they got back to the lab they went to what used to be Eddie's lab, now a lady named Julie worked there. Julie was a four year veteran, who had transferred from Los Angeles a few weeks before Eddie died. She had bright hazel eyes, and slightly tan skin, her strawberry blonde hair that usually bounced down to her shoulders was tied up in a ponytail.

"Hey," she said when she saw them walk in. "What can I help you with today?"

"We need some help getting some DNA from this hair that we found, and to see if anything comes up on this thumbprint that we also found."

"Alright," she said, taking the hair sample. "I can get this to you by the end of the day, and I can match up the print right now."

"Great," Max said, giving her the thumb print.

"Alright, let's see what we can get." She scanned the thumb print into AFIS (Automated Fingerprint Integrated System) and they watched the prints fly by. After about thirty seconds, it stopped and **13 possible matches found** came up.

"Now, lets isolate a different section," Julie said as she highlighted another ridge.

The prints flew by and **2 possible matches found** came up. "Alright," Julie said printing off the files of the people. "That should be a little easier."

"Ok then," Barry said. "Time to get rid of one of them." Barry leaned down and looked at the prints with a magnifying glass. The prints were pretty close and Barry was still fairly inexperienced, "Max, I can't tell, can you take a look at them?"

Max leaned back up five minutes later, "That's a tough call, I can't tell which one isn't a match, they both look the same," he said.

"Let me take a look," David said, leaning back down. Ten minutes later, David leaned back up. "Yeah that really is a tough call."

"I know how we can help narrow it down," Max said.

"How?" David asked.

"We could look up their criminal records," Max said. "One might be clean enough that we can cancel it out as a possible match."

"Alright," Barry said, "Who's the first suspect?"

"A Joe Dawson," Max said, as Julie ran his name. His file came up a few seconds.

"OK," Julie said, reading the file out loud as they read over her shoulder. "Joe Dawson, born June first, nineteen seventy-six. That makes him twenty-eight, twenty-nine in June. He committed his first crime at ten." She looked a little closer. "Damn, armed robbery at ten, spent six months in Juvenile Hall, then the day he got out, he stole a car and committed vehicular manslaughter. Spent another three years in Juvi. He stayed under the radar for the next two years, In ninety-one, he was convicted of rape and attempted murder. That sent him to Juvi for another three years and

six months in jail. In ninety-two he was
convicted of reckless driving, and driving
without a license. They gave him six months
probation. He stayed clean for three years
until ninety-five when he was charged with
possession of illegal firearms at a routine
traffic stop, went to jail for another five
years. Then in two thousand two, he was
suspected of murder, but that went nowhere."

"Damn," Max said. "I don't even think that
we need to check the other person's
background."

"I don't think so either," David said.
"But you can never be too careful."

"Who's next?" Julie asked.

"Her name is Maria Litch," Max said, as
her file came up.

"Maria Litch," Julie said. "Born March
second, nineteen sixty-three. Only thing here
is a speeding ticket in ninety-nine."

"That it?" Barry said.

"Yep," she said closing the file. "Besides
that, her file is spotless."

"Max," David said urgently. "We should
really get those notes or whatever they are
open."

"You're right, we should do that," Max
said. "Julie, could we get a print out of Joe's
record so we can get a warrant?"

"Sure," she said, as her fingers flew all
over the keyboard, in less than ten seconds his
file was in the printer. She grabbed it out and
handed it to Max. "Here you go."

"Thanks," Max said as they left.

"We should get this to Sid as soon as
possible," David said. "We might be able to get
a warrant by the end of the day."

"Alright," Barry said. "I could help get
the warrant."

"No, but thanks," David said. "I think I

will, you should stay here with Max, and help with the notes."

"Oh, OK," Barry said, a little disappointed. "Yeah, I can do that."

"Sorry if you are disappointed," David said, in a caring, but serious voice. "Again, I think you should stay here with Max, you could use some extra practice in the lab, get better on processing evidence. You already helped us get a warrant, no need to come with."

Then they went on their way.

Max and Barry went towards the lab, while David left for the warrant.

When Max and Barry got to the lab, they opened the evidence bags and took out the wet papers. Then they snapped on gloves, and took out tweezers and magnifying glasses, "Let's get started," Max said, as he attempted to unfold the paper as carefully as he could.

Max got the first piece of paper open in two minutes, there was a trace of writing on the soaked parchment, but Max couldn't tell by just looking at it. He grabbed a magnifying glass and saw four nearly washed away letters: 1**KEE**.

"1KEE?" Max said confused, "What does that mean?" Max look up at Barry. "Can you take a look at this, and make sure that I am reading this right?"

"Sure," Barry said, taking the magnifying glass. "No problem."

Barry looked down for about thirty seconds. "Yeah, it says 1KEE." He gave the magnifying glass back to Max. "Does that mean anything to you?"

"No," Max said. "I already said that, but whatever these things mean we must have to put them in order."

"Oh," Barry said. "Must not have heard."

"It's Ok," Max said. "Let's take a look at

the other papers, maybe the rest of the papers
will help us make sense of this."

Max was just as careful when he was
unfolding the second sheet. The second sheet
looked just like the first. Soaked, with
smeared almost ineligible letters, except there
were only two this time. Max could make out the
letters: 2**PX**.

"2PX!" Max said, more confused than the
first time. "That makes even less sense than
before."

"I bet we can assume that the rest of them
are going to make very little sense as well,"
Barry said, helping Max photograph them and put
them back in bags.

Max opened the third of the familiarly
soaked, nearly illegible letters. Like the
first, there were three letters: 3**ЕГN**.

"3ETN?" Max said. "That makes just as
little sense as the first two."

"What does any of those letters have to do
with this?" Barry asked.

"This might be another one of his little
games," Max said. "He may be toying with us, to
buy more time to do something, or there might
be some kind of message or something in the
random assortment of letters."

"Like what?" Barry said.

"I don't know," Max said. "Maybe a place,
or a person, or some kind of message, like I
said earlier. Probably something like that."

"Oh," Barry said, giving Max the last bag
and photographing and re-bagging the previous
note. "Let's see if the last note will make any
sense of the code."

"Fat chance," Max said. "It will probably
just make the whole thing more confusing."

"You never know," Barry said.

"Yeah," Max said. "You're probably right;
there might be a little chance."

Most likely not

Max opened the fourth just as carefully as the last three, and found himself looking at the same code. This time the letters were: 4APO.

"4APO?" Max said. "Nothing to it, just a bunch of letters, do you see any pattern, Barry?"

"Apo could be a name," Barry said.

"Yeah, David said it could be," Max said. "Do you see anything else?"

"Nope," Barry said. "but let me take a closer look, just in case." He took the bags and looked at the notes again. "**KEE, PX, EΓN,** and **APO,**" Barry said thinking. "Took, EEE, could mean 'me' PNK, could be someone's initials. This could be Took me something, or Me took someone."

"Yeah, that actually makes sense that that he took someone, like their life, or he kidnapped someone, or he wants to be taken, like he wants to be caught, which I'm pretty sure he or she wants to be at this point, but that still does not explain the numbers." Max said.

"Yeah, I am lost on that."

"We should meet back up with David later he might see something that we do not."

"Yeah," Barry said, agreeing with Max. "We should call him and see how the warrant is going."

"I was thinking the same thing," Max said, as he flipped out his cell phone and dialed up David.

David got to the D.A.'s office around the same time that Max opened the first note, discovering the new game that The Spade had left them. He walked in to the familiar surroundings that he had come to know well over

his years as a CSI. He has only known two DA's;
Kevin had been around the longest. There were
times that he argued to the point of insanity
over the amount of evidence needed for a
warrant. This time David was sure that there
was going to be no need for negotiation, the
evidence was good enough to get a warrant. But
on the other hand the intern DA, Ryan, who had
taken over when Kevin died, was still fuming
about the warrant they had gotten.

David walked over to the D.A.'s secretary.
She looked like she had seen more cases than
David. She had shoulder length gray hair that
was tied back in a pony tail. Her face had deep
wrinkles, and crows eyes that were darker than
space. They made her blue eyes seem brighter
than they were.

She looked up at David when he got to her
desk. "Can I help you with something?"

"Yeah," David said. "I need to see Mr.
Fird about a warrant."

"Well," she said in a preppy sarcastic
voice. "He is extremely busy. So you can give
me your name and number and he will get back to
you."

"Yeah," David said. "Like I'm going to
fall for that. If I leave right now, you're
probably going to lose the message and he won't
get back to me. What's he so busy with anyway."

"That is none of your business," she said.

"Well you know what?" Sid said from behind
him. "Eleven counts of murder just made it *our*
business."

She just stared at Sid for a second, then
she picked up the phone.

"Sir, Mr. Walker and Mr. Smith are here to
see you." She listened for a moment. "OK sir,
yes sir, I'll tell them." She put her phone
back down. "Take a seat over there," she
pointed to a section of chairs against the

opposite wall. "and he will be right with you."

"Thanks," Sid said, as they walked over and sat down.

"What took you so long?" David asked. "I didn't think that she was going to let me in."

"I got stuck in traffic," Sid said. "But I *got* here, didn't I? I *got* us in, didn't I?"

"Yeah," David said. "But if the D.A. is in as good as a mood as his secretary." David saw her staring at him, he gave a smile and a little wave. "We are in some serious trouble, and we have never met this one yet. He looked like a real dick when we ran into him while we were getting the fake warrant for Walter and Iva."

Before they got in, Max called, "Walker," David said, answering his phone.

"Hey David, its Max."

"Yeah," David said. "I read the caller ID, what's up?"

"Not much," Max said. "Barry and I opened the papers and found a code."

"What kind?" David said intrigued.

"I don't quite know yet," Max said. "We think it might be a message or something, Barry thinks that he figured it out."

"Oh yeah," David said. "What does he think that it means?"

"He thinks that it might be a message like 'took me PNK' or 'me took PNK'."

"PNK?" David said confused. "What is PNK?"

"We think that it may be someone's initials."

"So it is saying that he took someone with the initials PNK, and the other well, what does the other possible message mean?"

"We think that he is trying to say that he is PNK, another piece of evidence proving that he or she wants to be caught."

"Of course," David said. "Took me, like

take me."

"Yeah," Max said. "That's what we got out of it too."

"So that might give us a little help if we find someone with the initials PNK," David said.

"What was that guy's name again that we found today."

"Ummm..." David checked the file he had in his hand. "A Joe Dawson."

"Ah, crap," Max said. "That would have helped if he had the initials PNK."

"Yeah, well maybe the possible woman suspect has those initials," David said.

"Yeah, maybe," Max said. "By the way, did you get the warrant yet?"

"Nope, not yet," David said. "Still waiting."

"Alright," Max said. "Just give me a call when you get it so Barry and I can meet you there."

"Alright, can do," David said. "Bye."

"Bye."

David hung up and sat back down next to Sid. "How much longer do you think that it's going to be?"

"I don't know," Sid said becoming annoyed. "It better be soon, or we might have to just barge in, he isn't as busy as she says he is."

"Yeah tell me about it," David said.

No sooner had David finished, the door to the D.A.'s office opened.

"Speak of the devil," David said, as they stood up and walked towards the office.

As they walked over they saw a lady walk out. She was a fairly pretty lady in her early to mid-thirties. She had light brown hair that went down past her shoulders to her mid-back. Her eyes were a dazzling green.

"Is that his wife?" Sid whispered to Sid.

"No," David said. "No band on the finger."

"Well," Sid said, with a little snicker. "Isn't that a bitch?"

Next Ryan, the D.A. walked out laughing. He didn't notice that David and Sid were outside; he gave the mystery woman a little kiss. Then he noticed David and Sid standing across the hall.

"I'll..." he said urgently. "I'll get back to you." He moved the woman the other way. He flipped his pony tail back and held out a hand, "Mr. Walker, Mr. Smith, what can I do for you today?"

"We would like to talk to you about a warrant," Sid said. "Do you think that you can help us?"

"Well," Ryan said. "Why don't you step into my office, and I'll see what I can do."

Ryan's office was full of pictures of his family. He sat down behind his desk, as David and Sid sat in front of him. "Can I get you anything to drink? Water? Soda?"

"I'll have some water," David said.

"Tea would be nice if you have it."

"Certainly," Ryan picked up his phone. "Martha? Could you bring in two waters and a tea please?" There was a slight pause. "Thank you," he said.

"What kind of warrant do you need?" Kevin asked. "Search? Arrest?"

"Arrest," David said. "We have a suspect in the Spade case."

"Oh, yeah?" Ryan said. "Now this isn't a fake one again, is it? Do you want to make another pathetic attempt at trying to save the victims."

That was beyond what David could take. "What the fuck is your problem?" David demanded.

"Excuse me?" Ryan said, a little shocked.

"You heard me, you little prick," David said in a tone that Sid had never heard before. "What is your problem?"

"Well..." Kevin said.

"We tried to do one little thing, we tried to save two innocent human beings, who did nothing wrong, and were killed in part of someone's sick little game. When we came down here a few months ago, and your predecessor helped us with the fake warrant and we thought that you would have done the same. Kevin was a good man, and it was a damn shame that you had to take his place. For a moment I actually thought that you had the smallest thing of something that might be considered a soul. This little act of what seems like a miscue in your face is sickening, how can you even mock someone's attempt at trying to save a life?"

Ryan was speechless.

David on the other hand had plenty more to say, "Now when we actually need a legit warrant, you make a mockery of us. I demand an explanation, an apology, and a warrant."

Martha cleared her throat from behind, "Here are your drinks."

"Thank you," they all said as they took their drinks.

As soon as Martha went back outside they started talking again.

"Well I don't think that I owe you two of those things, but depending on how the next few minutes go, I might not give you any of those things," Ryan said. "Show yourself worthy."

David was about to explode again, and Sid could sense that, he put his hand on David's shoulder, "Why don't you let me do the talking."

David started to object, but Ryan interrupted, "Yeah, just let him do the talking, wouldn't want to dig your grave any deeper, now would you? My advice would be to stop right now while you still have a chance to get back up." Ryan waited for a reaction, when he saw David ease back in his chair, he finished. "Sid, go on what do you know?"

"Well sir," he said. "We have very good evidence linking Mr. Dawson to the latest crime scene. His fingerprints were found on the head board where the female was tied."

"Are you sure that you have it right this time, and you will be able to catch him?"

"Yes sir, we are very confident in our ability to catch him."

"Will you be able to keep him *alive* long enough for enough questioning this time?"

Sid was starting to get annoyed, but he held back his anger, "Yes sir, we will keep him alive long enough to get anything out of him that he might know."

"Alright then," Ryan said. "Why don't you wait outside while I get your warrant?"

Sid and David got up and started to leave, "Wait Mr. Walker, I didn't say that you could leave, I want to have a little word with you first."

Sid left as David sat back down, "What do you need?"

Ryan waited until he was sure that Sid was away, "I think that you owe me an explanation for what just happened."

David sighed, there was nothing he could do, there was no use arguing any further with the D.A., he could lose his job, "I'm sorry sir, I just lost it when you didn't even care about what happened to the latest victims, and the fact that you mocked our attempt to save them. It was just the straw that broke the camel's back."

Ryan just stared at him for a second, "Well that was kind of an explanation, but it wasn't good enough, I think I am going to put in a complaint to get your badge taken."

"You go ahead and do that," David said. "But when you do, be prepared to go down with me."

"Excuse me?" Ryan asked surprised.

"I have more years as a CSI, and a respected member of the city, longer than you have been alive. I can make up a story about how you verbally abused me, and tried to physically attack me."

"Yeah," Kevin said. "Who's going to believe that?"

"I have a cop, and a good friend out there who heard you abuse me, and if he hadn't blocked you, I would have been assaulted."

Kevin said nothing.

"And to put the icing on the cake, I know that you have been having an affair, and in the office of one of Clarke Counties most respected late official?" David stood up and started to leave.

"Why did I call you back again?" Kevin said, playing stupid.

"I forgot my file," David said, going back to pick it up. "You have a nice day now," David said leaving.

"What about my lady friend?" Kevin asked.

"What lady?" David said as he opened the door.

David went back out where Sid was waiting for him. "What happened?"

"Nothing," David said. "Just forgot my file."

Sid started to laugh "You are one lucky son of a bitch, you know that, right?"

David just smiled.

Five minutes later Kevin came back out and gave them the warrant.

"Thanks," they both said as they left.

Before they got in their cars Sid said, "How did you get away with that outburst in there?"

"I told him that I would bring him down with me if he turned me in," David said. "And I said that I would tell his wife he was having an affair."

"You know that might have been his sister or something like that. Wouldn't you have felt stupid if it was?"

"I was very confident that he was having an affair because of three key things. One, he wouldn't kiss his sister like that."

"Oh, yeah," Sid said. "Missed that little detail."

"Two," David said. "He had lipstick on his collar."

"Another good reason that I am not a CSI," Sid said.

"And three," David said. "His shirt was messily buttoned as if redressing quickly."

"Oh," Sid said getting in.

"Hold on a minute," David said. "Let me call Max so he and Barry can meet us at his home."

"Alright," Sid said leaning back against his car.

Max picked up after two rings. "Levinton."

"Hey Max," David said. "We got the warrant. Want to help us deliver it?"

"Sure," Max said. "Where is his house?"

"It's actually at the MGM," David said. "The same place as the house of knives?"

"Yep, in the very next room."

They met up at the MGM fifteen minutes later. They went up to his floor, and headed for his room.

Sid pulled out his gun and leaned up

against the door. "Mr. Dawson, open up."

He waited a few minutes.

"Mr. Dawson, L.V.P.D. please open up."

He waited a few more minutes, nothing.

He look back at Max, Barry, and David, "Stand back, I'm going in."

He gave one last warning, "Mr. Dawson please open up or I'm coming in."

Nothing. Sid backed up, and slammed his shoulder into the door.

The door went down and they went in.

"L.V.P.D.!" Sid yelled.

A woman screamed from one of the rooms. They followed it as fast as they could, fearing the worst.

They got to the room and found nothing, just a lady laying in bed with a man.

"What the fuck?" the man said, holding up his hands. "Did I do something?"

"Are you a Joe Dawson?" Sid asked.

"No," he said. "My name is Frank Deed."

Sid did not look convinced.

"Here," he said reaching in the side drawer. "Look at my license."

The man was right, he was not Joe Dawson.

"Sorry about the inconvenience," Sid said as they left.

"Shit," Sid said. "How could we have made a mistake like this?"

"We rushed into it," Max said. "But we had the right to; he could have been killing someone."

"Yeah, don't worry about it," Barry said. "Everyone makes mistakes."

They were leaving when Barry noticed the man checking out at the front desk, "Hey guys," he said, waiting till he had their attention. "Isn't that him right there checking out?"

"Where?" Max said. "There must be like twenty people over there checking out or in."

"Right over there in the middle of the line," Barry said pointing.

"Please," Sid said, beginning to plea. "Please Barry be more specific."

"He is in the middle of the line," Barry said more slowly. "He is wearing a blue suit, he has red hair that is hardly sticking out from under his cowboy hat."

They waited a few minutes, and he turned around, and made eye contact with them. He turned back causally, stepped out of line, and walked the other way.

"Son of a bitch," Sid said. "That's him."

The man walked out and they ran after him. Sid pulled out his gun, "Mr. Dawson freeze."

Nothing, he cocked his gun, but he had lost him.

"Damn," Sid said putting his gun away.

"He's outside," Max said pointing.

They all ran out after him. When they got out the door he was getting in his car.

"L.V.P.D. freeze!" Sid yelled, pulling his gun back out.

Joe heard nothing as he started his car.

Sid was about to charge his car from behind when the car exploded, and sent Max, David, Sid, and Barry flying back towards the hotel.

They watched helplessly as the remainder of the car landed, still on fire. As Barry tried to stand back up, he saw the reminder of their only suspect, blown away like the first.

28

The Wreckage

After about five minutes, the ringing stopped. Barry could hear sirens coming closer to the hotel.

How could this have happened?

"Barry?" Max called. "Barry? Are you OK?"

"What?" Barry said, his ears not completely back to normal.

"Are you OK?" Max said a little louder.

"Yeah," Barry said, starting to stand up. "Yeah I'm fine."

Barry dug his pinky into his ear, trying to clear it out. Nothing happened. Barry dug a little deeper, desperate to get his hearing all the way back. Nothing.

"What's wrong?" Max asked.

"My ear," Barry said nervously. "I'm having a little trouble hearing."

"Oh," Max said calmly. "That's normal after a loud noise, mine is a little off too."

"Where are David and Sid?" Barry asked with concern in his voice.

"They're right over there." Max said, as he pointed behind Barry.

Barry looked behind him and saw David and Sid sitting on the floor, beginning to get up and dust themselves off as well. Barry got up as well, glass falling off him as he did, "Is anyone hurt?" he asked.

"I don't think so," Max said. "Luckily not too many people were close to the car when it blew up, I think there are quite a few who got knocked off their feet as we did."

The police cars, fire trucks, and ambulances showed up a few minutes later. Before the questioning began on them, they were taken to the ambulances to be checked out. Sid was fine, besides the cut on his leg. Max had nothing wrong with him, neither did David. When Barry was checked out, his hearing was still not back to normal.

Barry was concerned, "The car exploded about ten minutes ago, and my hearing still hasn't returned to normal," he said. "Should I be worried?"

How could this have happened?

The paramedic that was checking him out was a man who appeared to be in his early fifties, his ghost white hair was neatly combed over his face, barely scarred by the devil known as time, "No, it should start to improve by tomorrow, but it still could mean nothing if it hasn't. Has it improved the smallest little bit, if you know?"

"I don't really know," Barry said, feeling a little better. "My ears were ringing for about the first five minutes maybe."

"Well, the fact that the ringing has stopped and you can still hear is a good thing," Barry looked a little confused. "Sometimes if your ears are ringing for a long period of time, you can lose all your hearing."

"OK," Barry said. "What if it doesn't improve?"

"If it doesn't improve by this time tomorrow, I highly recommend that you see a doctor, to prevent further injury."

"Thanks," Barry said, as he got up and walked over to where Max, Sid, and David were being questioned.

When he got over, they started on him too,

"What happened?"

"Well," Barry said. "We were here to arrest Mr. Dawson..."

"Dawson," the cop said, writing down the name. "Is that the name of the man who was in the car at the time of the explosion?"

"Yes sir," Barry said.

"Go on," the cop said twirling his hand.

"We were chasing after him, and he refused to stop when we told him to," Barry said. "Sid was about to shoot his leg to bring him down, when he hopped in his car and blew up. The blast knocked us off our feet and sent us back towards the hotel. If the blast had been any bigger, it could have been a lot worse."

"Anything else you need to tell me?" the cop asked.

Barry thought about the hotel room they busted into. He could see Sid behind the cop. He must have heard the question, or seen the conflict in Barry's eyes, he gave a quick shake of his head.

"No sir," Barry said. "That's it."

"Thank you," the cop said as he got back into his cruiser and left.

Barry walked back over to Sid, David, and Max, they were still in as much shock as he was, "Have they cleared the scene yet?" Barry asked.

"Almost," Max said. "And they are sending us over some tools too."

"Do you guys have any idea who could have done this?" Sid asked.

"I think it might have been the other person who is helping them," Barry said. "Richard said that there was two men."

"So one of them just decided that he was no longer needed?" Sid asked.

"Exactly," Barry said. "He was just like Richard, another weak link in the chain."

"But Richard killed himself," David said.

"Yeah, but do you remember what he said before he pulled the trigger?" Barry asked.

"No," they all said.

"He said something about how strong and smart they were." Barry saw that none of them recalled. "He might have pulled the trigger, but they had caused it by all the manipulation they did to him. They got inside his head and caused him to crack. Thus getting rid of the first weak link, the most likely to cave in."

"So they thought that this guy was going to talk too?" David asked.

"Yeah," Barry said. "that's what I think they are doing. They planted the print on the boat on purpose, and then they probably convinced him to get out, that we were getting closer."

"So then they blow him up?" Sid said.

"Yep," Max said. "No more weak link."

"Exactly," Barry said.

A cop came up. "Mr. Levinton, Mr. Walker?"

"Yes," they both said.

"The scene is secured, you can check it out now," he told them.

"Thank you." David said.

"Thanks," Max repeated.

They all walked over to the remainder of the car. The car looked like it used to be nice. They could see the remainder of a BMW emblem in the front. David started to take pictures of the car and surrounding scene, as Max, Barry, and Sid looked around the scene. They couldn't do much, they didn't have their tools yet, or even any gloves. They could still feel a little bit of heat rising up from the wreckage.

How could this have happened?

Five minutes later when their tools were dropped off, they got started. First, they waited for David to finish taking pictures, and for Larry to pick up the remainder of the body. When David finished taking pictures, they only had to wait a few more minutes for Larry to pick up the body. The body smelled worse than anything that Barry had ever smelled. The skin was fried and nearly melted off. It took a little longer than usual to get the body out, it was stuck to the seat.

"Let's try to get this guy out," Larry said. "Barry, can you give me a hand?"

"Umm," Barry said hesitantly. "Sure, yeah I'll help."

Barry snapped on some gloves and got a hold of part of the body. He started to try to get it off the seat, when the body broke from the hip down.

Barry gasped, and jumped back. The legs flew up and hit the ground and broke again. "Oh, my God!" Barry said horrified. "Larry, I'm so sorry, I..."

"Don't worry about it," Larry said calmly.

Barry couldn't calm down, "I have to worry about it, I mean I just broke the body, I..."

Larry interrupted him again, "Barry, it's OK," he said in a comforting voice, while he put his hand on Barry's shoulder trying to calm him down, "It could have happened to anyone."

Barry was mortified almost to the point of tears, "But it didn't, it happened to me, I just wrecked the body more than it had to be."

"Barry listen," Larry said, still trying to calm the kid. "It is not you fault, it would have happened to me if I had the other half, OK?"

"Yeah," Barry said holding it back. "I...I just need to go get some rest for a few minutes."

"OK," Max said. "take your time."

"Thanks," Barry said walking back towards

the hotel.

"Whoa, that kid is pretty darn dedicated," Larry said.

"Yeah," David said. "He is going to be one hell of an investigator."

"I agree," Max said.

When Larry left a few minutes later, and Barry came back, they were able to start examining the scene more closely.

"Alright," Barry said. "What do we do here? I've never handled an explosion before."

"Well the first thing I think we should do, is find the bomb, in case there is a part of it that hasn't exploded yet." David said.

"Why would there be a part that hasn't exploded yet?" Barry asked.

"I can't explain it too well, but basically it's like those bombs from World War Two that they keep finding," he said. "I don't think that there is any part that didn't explode, but I don't know much about bombs, I don't want to take a chance."

"Shouldn't we just call in the bomb squad?" Barry asked.

"Yeah," David said. "That is a pretty good idea, I don't want to get blown up."

After much deliberation, David convinced the bomb squad to come down. When they got there they asked about where they thought the bomb was.

Barry answered, "I'm pretty sure that it came from the bottom of the car."

"OK," the head guy said. "I'll check it out, stand back."

He took out the little camera that looks like a little tube, and slid it under the car. He took it out a few minutes later.

"You're fine," he said, packing back up. "It looks like it was a standard pipe bomb."

"How can you tell?" Barry asked, intrigued.

"I've been in this business for almost fifteen years, I know a pipe bomb when I see one, even if it is in pieces," he said annoyed. "Plus the end cap is still on the bottom."

"Oh," Barry said, disappointed.

"Thanks for coming," David said.

"Yeah, whatever," he replied without even looking back.

"Dick," Barry said, when he was out of ears reach.

"Yeah," David. "I've never really liked that guy."

"Me either," Max said. "So, shall we get started now?"

"Yeah," David replied. "We got some work ahead of us, we better get started."

"We should get the end cap," Barry suggested.

"No, we should wait until we get back to the lab to take anything off the car," Max said. "Just take a look around the scene."

"And bag what you find."

"OK," Barry said, as he got started.

There were little pieces of the car and bomb all around the parking lot. Barry started to bag. After about five minutes, Barry already had twenty-five bags of pieces of metal. He went back for more and got started again. The whole thing was exhilarating to Barry. It was like a giant puzzle to him. Except there was no drawing to show what it was supposed to look like. That fact made it all the more exciting for Barry, he loved a challenge. After about ten more minutes, Barry was sure that he found all the pieces in his little ten foot radius. He put away his bags and got started on the next little part of the parking lot. The next part of the lot took him twenty minutes. Barry

started to check the next part, when he felt a
little poke on the top of his head. He brushed
his hair with his hand to see what it was.

There was nothing.

Barry went back to work. A few seconds
later, he felt another prick. He put his hand
up again, and a drop of water fell on his hand.
Barry looked up realizing the horrible truth.
The sky was blacker than the ace of spades.
Lightning flashed across the sky, a few seconds
later the thunder shook the parking lot, and
the sky opened up.

"Shit!" Barry heard David yell.

"Get as much as you can!" Barry heard Sid
scream.

They all ran across the parking lot
grabbing as much as they could.

When they had bagged all that they saw
they ran back to the truck. That was when Barry
saw it. It was a little piece of what looked
like the pipe being carried down towards a
drain pipe.

The bomb

Barry jumped out of the car and chased
after it.

"Barry," Max yelled through the storm.
"What are you doing?"

Barry didn't answer, he just kept going
forward determined to get the piece of bomb. He
was getting closer; he could almost reach out
and grab it.

The pipe neared the drain and he feared
the worst. Barry dove out and tried to grab it;
however, gravity pushed Barry into the curb and
he felt helplessly as the pipe slipped from his
fingers and down the drain.

29

Orange Creek

The rain went on for fifteen more minutes.

"Alright now," the paramedic said. "Your nose isn't broken, just apply some pressure for a few minutes, and the bleeding should stop."

"Thanks," it came out 'fanks'.

Max and David approached him, "You alright?" Max asked.

"Yeah," Barry said. "I'm fine."

"Why did you jump out of the car like that?" David asked.

Barry checked the tissue, the blood had stopped. "I saw part of the bomb being washed away, I thought I would be able to catch it."

"Oh," Max said. "What did it look like?"

"It was part of a pipe," Barry said. "Almost like a little cup." He made the shape with his hand."

"Thanks," David said. "We might be able to get a pretty good sketch off that."

"And we might be able to get some stuff from this." Sid said rolling up a bag.

"What's that?" Max asked.

"Mr. Dawson's luggage, thanks to the cooperation of the employees of the MGM," he said.

"Sweet," Barry said. "let's check it out."

They brought it over the car, put it on the hood and opened it up. Inside they found nothing out of the ordinary. Some clothes, a few maps, and some poker chips. They shifted through the stuff and then found something that stuck out as strange. It was one of those *For Dummies* books, but that wasn't the strange part. It was on Greek.

"What the?" Max said.

"Why would he need a book on Greek?"

Barry thought for a minute, and the lights came on, "Max, remember that code thing that he left us?"

"Yeah," Max said. "You think it is Greek?"

"I do," Barry said. "And now that I am thinking about it, I don't think that 'T' is a 'T'."

"What?" Max said confused.

"I think that I remember that that 'T' looked like it was missing part of its head."

"OK," Max said slowly, still not entirely sure what Barry was talking about.

Barry got in the car, "I'll explain it more when we get back to the lab."

They got back to the lab five minutes later, and went straight to Max's office. Max got out the papers that had the codes on them.

He put them on the table, "Now what were you saying about the head of the 'T' being missing?"

Barry searched through the pieces of paper until he found the one he was looking for. "Look," he said, pointing to the one with the letters 'ΕΓΝ' "You see how the 'T' doesn't have a left head?"

They looked a little closer. "No I don't see it, it still looks like a 'T' to me." Max said.

Barry sighed and covered the 'E'. "Look," he said, annoyed and angry.

Now the paper read: 'ΓΝ'.

"Oh," David said surprised. "I see it."

Barry looked over to Max. "Do you?"

"Yeah," he said, a bit embarrassed. "I see it now."

"So what does it all mean?" David asked.

"I don't know *yet*," Barry said, pulling out the *Greek for Dummies* book. "But we are about to find out."

He opened the book to a list of the alphabet. "What's the first paper say?"

"**KEE**," Max said.

"Alright, that translates over to 'KEE'."

"Hope they are all that easy," David said.

"Me too," Barry said. "What's next?"

"**PX**" Max said.

"That goes over to 'RC'" Barry said.

"Next is **E** 'T' thing **N**," Max said.

"OK," Barry said. "Now we have EGN."

"And the last letters are," Max said.

"**APO**."

"Apo," Barry said. "That goes over to ARO."

"So what do we have?" Max said.

"KEERC EGNARO."

"Kerrc Egnaro?"

"What does that mean?" David asked, confused.

"I don't know," Barry said. "I think it's a name, might be the killer's."

"Or," David said. "It might be the name of his next victim."

"That's not what it means," Max said.

"What?" David said. "It's not?"

"What's it mean?" Barry wondered.

"It's Orange Creek spelled backwards," Max said nervously.

"Why is it spelled backwards?" David asked.

"I think I know," Max said, getting more nervous.

"What?" Barry asked.

"I think he is trying to tell us that to get to the end, we have to go back to the beginning," Max said, starting to shake a little. "We have to go back to the Creek."

"So the same guy who is doing this did
Orange Creek?" Barry asked. "I thought that
they caught and executed him."

"They did," David said. "But before you
came with Hallaway, and Dominic, I received a
call from him. The Orange Creek killer was his
best friend."

"You got a call from him?" Barry asked
confused.

"Yeah," David started to explain. "It was
just after we finished the second autopsies;
Max had left early because of complications. I
got a call from him and he knew about a lot of
the facts of the case that were never released
to the press. Than he revealed that it was all
Max's fault and he needed to pay."

"Whoa, that's some pretty serious shit,"
Barry said. "By the way, where is Hallaway?"

"I'm pretty sure he went home."

"Oh, that makes sense." Barry looked over
at Max. "What's wrong with Max?"

"Orange Creek was his first case, and it
took a lot out of him, he almost died trying to
catch the killer."

"Oh," Barry said surprised. "I didn't know
about that."

"Yeah," David said. "That was one of the
details that was never released."

"Damn," Barry said. "No wonder he's scared
about re-visiting this case."

"Yeah," David said. "It really got to
him." There was more than David was telling
Barry; the aftermath sent him into therapy for
about a year.

"Damn," Barry said. "Are you sure that he
will be able to handle this?"

"He should be fine," David said. "Just
give him a few minutes to regain his

composure."

"Alright," Barry said. "We can wait."

"Yeah," David said. "We have plenty of time."

They did not need any time at all; Max was ready in five minutes.

"Ok," Max said. "Let's go to storage, and see what we missed."

"Are you sure that you're ready?" David asked. "We can wait a little longer if you want."

"No," Max took a deep breath. "No, it's fine, let's do it."

"OK," David said. "Let's go get the evidence."

"Where is the evidence?" Barry asked intrigued.

"Oh yeah," David said, feeling stupid. "You haven't done that yet, have you?"

Barry shook his head, "Nope."

"Don't worry," Max said. "We will show you how to do it, it's actually quite easy."

They got to the evidence lockup a few minutes later. Barry waited with Max while David signed in.

"Let's go," David said, opening up the door.

The room was chilly causing a little shiver to go through Barry's body, "Why is it so cold in here?" Barry asked.

"So the evidence doesn't get compromised," Max said. "Just in case a situation like this comes up, or we get a new lead on a case that has gone cold."

"Here it is," David said, pulling down a box from the second shelf, handing it to Max, getting another, giving it to Barry, and grabbing another down. "Let's go check it out, and see what we can find."

They returned to the lab, and opened the

evidence boxes. There was nothing out of the
ordinary that came right out.

Barry was looking through the pictures and
evidence bags, "What are we supposed to be
looking for?"

"I don't quite know," Max said. "Just be
on the look out for anything out of the
ordinary."

Barry was still confused. *Like*?"

"I don't know," Max said, getting annoyed
for having to repeat himself. "Something like a
piece of evidence that we missed, or a..." Max
stopped and stared at a picture.

Barry looked over at him. "Max? Max?
What's wrong?"

"Or a person," Max said.

"What?" Barry and David both said,
surprised.

"Look," Max put the picture where they
could all see it, and pointed to a corner. "You
can just make out a leg on the left edge.

Barry and David peered over at the picture
where Max was pointing. Max was right. They
could just make out a leg, it looked like the
person was running away.

"Is that the killer?" Barry asked.

"I don't know," Max said confused.

"Why didn't we notice this before?" David
asked.

Max thought that he knew, "I bet we didn't
see it because we weren't looking for something
strange, and his leg looks like a little tree
at first glance."

"No," David said. "Why didn't we see this
when we were taking the pictures?"

Max was a little embarrassed, "I think I
can explain that too."

"What?" David asked.

Max started to explain, "I was a rookie,
and this was my first case..." Max paused. "I

didn't quite know how to completely work the camera, I was a little sloppy, I might have been trying to set it up when he ran away."

"Oh," Barry said. "So you could have caught the guy after the first murder?"

"Well, no," Max started to explain. "When we caught him he was taken completely by surprise, and he still almost got away. It was actually good that I was so sloppy with the camera, it saved my life."

Barry was curious of Max's view point, "How?"

"Well you *do* remember how the bodies were found?" Max asked.

"Yeah," Barry said. "They were all killed different, but the same detail was on each one they all had..." Barry suddenly realized Max's point. "*Oh.*"

"Yeah," Max said. "It would have been bad."

Five minutes later they had nothing. There was nothing out of the ordinary, besides the leg in the first picture.

"Maybe we should go to the crime scene," David said. "Maybe he left something there."

"Yeah," Max said, seeing his point. "Maybe he wants us to go *all* the way back."

When they got to the Creek, it looked very peaceful. There was no way anyone could tell that at one time it held the clues to one of the worst crimes in history.

Barry read the sign, "Honey Creek? I thought it was

Orange?"

"No, no," Max said. "They started to call it Orange Creek because the water turned from brown to a shade of orange when the blood hit it."

"Oh," Barry said. "Do you know why it is called Honey?"

"Simple." David went to the edge and picked up a honey suckle. "It is surrounded by honey suckles."

"Oh," Barry felt stupid for not noticing the suckles growing all around the edges. "Do you see anything?"

"No," Max replied. "But that does not mean a thing, he isn't going to make this easy for us if there actually is anything out here."

So they started to look around, looking for anything that didn't belong.

Barry tripped over a small tree, catching himself in the nick of time, "Damn," he said, getting up and brushing himself off, he turned around and looked at the unscarred tree. There was something about the tree that was bugging him, but he couldn't quite put his finger on it. He went back out to the edge of the woods, and looked at it from a different view.

What is wrong with that tree?

He couldn't see anything different from his new view, so he went back to where Max and David were.

"You find anything?" Max asked him.

"No," he answered.

"How about you David?" Max asked.

David jumped back from the other side of the Creek, "No, I didn't find anything."

They started back up the hill, when a slight breeze came over them. Barry noticed that the tree did not move an inch.

What is wrong with that tree?

When they got back up the hill, Barry figured it out.

"Max," he said. "I found something."

"What?"

Barry pointed to the tree, "That's not a tree."

Max didn't know what Barry was talking about, "What, oh course it is."

"No," Barry said. "I first knew that there was something wrong with it when I tripped over it, and it hardly moved. Then when that breeze came, it didn't move an inch. Finally, that tree is in one of the crime scene pictures, exactly the same size it is now."

Suddenly Max and David got it. "We should see what that tree *really* is."

Barry nodded, "Just what I was thinking."

They got some shovels and came back. They went down and started to dig up what appeared to be a tree. After about a minute they hit something hard, and started digging more franticly. What they found was unexpected. It was a briefcase.

Max picked it up. "What the hell?"

It was a simple briefcase, brown leather covering, brown handle and a coded lock.

"Damn," Max said. "Now we need a code."

"Wait," Barry said. "Don't touch it; it might be in the right sequence already."

Max lowered the suitcase and tried to push the locks open and to his surprise, it opened. Barry just smiled. Max set it down and lifted the lid. The contents of the suitcase surprised Max. There was a cell phone and a note.

"What?" Max said, picking up the phone and note. "How did this happen? He must have just recently put this here."

"What does the note say?" Barry asked, standing up.

Max opened the note, the letters were bold type written: **When the time is right, I will call.**

Max read it to Barry and David.

"When the time is right, I will call?" Barry repeated. "What does that mean?"

"I don't know," David said, turning to Max. "Do you have any ideas?"

"No," Max said. "I have no idea."

Barry thought about it again. *When the*

time is right, I will call. "I don't know what it means," he told them. "But I don't like the sound of it."

"I agree," David replied as he bagged and tagged the note. "But I do know whatever it turns out to be, it won't be good."

They all looked at each other, and for once they could not hide the fear from their eyes.

30

Cry For Help

Ron was at the front desk for the first time when he saw the man. From the time Ron was a little kid, he loved Vegas. The first time he visited Sin City, he was nine. Everything was amazing to him. The size of the hotels was breathtaking; he had never seen anything so big and the lights! They were in shapes and colors that he had never seen before. The insides of the hotel were just as breathtaking. He had never seen so many slots and games. After his trip was over he itched to go back.

When he was sixteen, he got his wish and went back. By this time he had grown into the man that he was today. He was ready this time, he had a fake I.D., and he was able to grow a full beard in two days. So a few days after he left he grew it out, the thickness of it covered his face, and he appeared to be in his thirties. He had the time of his life. He fooled all the people in the casinos, no one even bothered to check his I.D. when he ordered drinks. By the end of the trip, he was hooked. He just had to live there. The will of it drove him deeper into his studies, and when he was in eleventh grade, he got a full scholarship to LVU. So he got his wish, and he moved to Vegas. When he was in his senior year of college, he got a job at the MGM. He was moving up fast. He had only been a bellboy for three weeks. Now he worked at the desk, and knew within a few years, he was going to own the place. He still had his head in the clouds when the man came up to the desk.

He looked up at him, "Hi sir, how are you doing?"

The man stood there for a moment like he was not sure how to answer. When he did his voice had the rough sandpaper quality of Clit Eastwood, "Good, thank you."

Ron smiled at him, "Is there anything that I can do for you today?"

Again, there was a long pause from the man, "Could you help me find a friend?"

"Sure," Ron turned to his computer. "What is your friend's name?"

He didn't pause this time, "Barry Johnson."

"Barry Johnson." Ron repeated. He had seen Barry earlier in the day, when that bomb went off. "He's not here right now, can I take a message for him?"

"Actually, do you think that you can let me into his room?" He waited for a reply.

"I can't do that sir," Ron replied.

"Please," the man said in a desperate voice. "Today is his birthday, and I would like to surprise him."

"Sir," he repeated. "I'm sorry, but I can't do that."

"Come on, you can let it slide." The man slid something towards him. "His other friend Benjamin says that it is OK, and he wants to get to know you too."

Ron slid the bill back, "Sorry, no can do."

The man put another C-note on the desk and slid them both towards Ron.

Ron shook his head.

The man slid a third bill onto the desk, "Come on."

Ron reluctantly took the bills, he didn't get tips anymore. "Let me show you to his room." He took the key from behind the desk. "Follow me."

He led the man up to Barry's room, and unlocked the door. "No one is to know about this," he said sternly. "Got it?"

"Know about what?" The man played stupid.

Ron laughed. "Thanks, you have a good day now, Mr.?"

"Frank," the man said going into the room. "Ben Frank."

When the time is right, I will call. Barry could not get those words out of his head. *When the time is right, I will call.* Barry didn't want to think about what the killer had up his sleeve this time. It was all too much, and he was glad that the day was over. Max and David dropped him off at about seven o'clock. As he was going to the elevator, the desk clerk stopped him.

"Hi," he said. "How are you doing tonight, Mr. Johnson?"

"Good how are you?"

"Very good, thanks for asking."

Barry got in the elevator, when he realized he didn't have his key. He jumped back out and went back to the desk clerk. "Sorry," he said. "I left my key in my room, could I have a spare?"

"Oh," the desk clerk said. "Don't worry about it, you friend is waiting for you, he got..." the clerk stopped.

"Got what?"

"Sorry," he said. "I wasn't supposed to tell you, he wanted to surprise you."

Barry was curious. "What's his name?"

The desk clerk thought for a minute. "Frank." he paused. "I don't remember his first name."

Barry thought he knew who he was talking about, his friend Kent Frank from back home, "Don't worry," Barry said, as he went back towards the elevator. "I know who it is."

Barry was extremely excited. He hadn't seen Kent since he left for law school; he must have just gotten out. He went up to his room and knocked on the door. "Kent," he said. "Let me in man."

Nothing.

Barry repeated. "Kent, let me in."

Still, there was nothing.

Barry knocked a little harder, the door creaked open. A shiver went down Barry's spine; Kent didn't do things like this. He slowly walked in. "Kent, where are you?"

The room was silent.

"Kent, stop this, it's not funny anymore."

Barry heard the door close behind him; he turned around and saw nothing. He heard a noise behind him but before he had a chance to turn around, a hand covered his mouth.

Barry started to panic, when another hand covered his mouth with a damp cloth. Barry stared to feel faint. In the moments before he passed out, the thought in his head suddenly became crystal clear.

When the time is right, I will call.
When the time is right, I will call.
When the time is right, I will call...

Max got home at eight. Like Barry, he was exhausted. A whole lot of shit had happened today. They were at a dead end. When the day started he thought that they were close to getting another suspect in the case. They had him and then, boom, back at square one. They had nothing.

Max walked in the door, and went to the fridge to see what was for dinner. He looked on the first shelf, and found some meatloaf and some mashed potatoes. Max took it out and heated it up. While it was heating he poured himself a glass of milk and picked up the newspaper. He had just started to glance at the headlines when his wife came down.

She kissed him and rubbed his back a little, "Hi, honey." She sat down beside him. "How was your day?"

Max put the paper down, "Did you hear about the MGM?"

"Yeah," she said.

"Well that was our guy."

"Oh, what else happened?"

"I'd rather not talk about it." Max picked the newspaper back up.

Sue knew that something was very wrong, Max always told her what was on his mind, "Come on honey." She started rubbing his back. "You can tell me."

"No," Max said, resisting. "I *really* don't want to talk about it; I had a really bad day." He put down the paper. "On another note, how was your day?"

Sue shrugged. "Same old, same old."

"I was thinking that I would go to bed early tonight, I'm worn out."

"Yeah," Sue agreed. "That sounds like a good idea."

Max had just started to dose off, when the phone rang.

He leaned over and picked it up, "Hello?" he said sleepily.

"Max Levinton?" asked a voice that Max didn't recognize.

He sat up. "Yeah?"

"My name is Greg Deaton; I am the supervisor on the night shift."

Max rubbed his eyes, starting to wake up a little more, *"Ok."*

"I was checking in evidence tonight, and something in your box started ringing.

Max was now fully awake, "Excuse me?"

Greg repeated himself, "There is something ringing in your evidence box."

When the time is right, I will call.

"What did you do?" Max asked.

"Nothing, I called you as soon as it happened," he said.

"Thanks." Max began to get dressed. "I'll be right over."

"OK," Greg said. "Is there anything else I should do?"

Max thought for a moment, "Did you call David and Barry."

"I already called David, and he told me to call Barry too. I don't have his number." He paused. "Who is Barry?"

"Long story," Max said.

"Alright," he said. "No need to explain."

"Bye."

"Bye."

Max got in his car fearing the worst.

When the time is right, I will call.

David got home at about eight thirty. Max had gone home early, and he checked the phone into evidence. On the way home he stopped at McDonalds, and picked up a Big Mac meal. He threw it on his table when he got home. He ate his meal in silence, thinking about what had happened today. His Mac was gone in under a minute, he hadn't realized how hungry he was. When his fries were gone, he was still hungry. He checked his cabinet and found a half full bag of Doritos. He sat down and finished off the bag. He took a shower, and went to bed.

David had been asleep for about ten minutes when his phone rang.

What? It's too late for someone to be calling. David leaned over and saw the clock, it was only ten-thirty.

He got up, and answered his phone.

"Hello?"

"David Walker?" An unfamiliar voice asked.

"Yeah."

"My name is Greg Deaton, I am the supervisor on the night shift."

David didn't see where this was going, "*Yeah.*"

"I was in the evidence room just now, and something in your evidence box started ringing.

When the time is right, I will call.

"Did you open it?"

"No sir, it's still ringing as we speak."

"Great, I'll be right over."

"Do you want me to call Mr. Levinton?"

"That would be great, and Barry too, if it's not too much trouble."

"Who's Barry?"

"Never mind, I'll call him."

"Alright then."

"Bye."

"Bye."

David knew exactly what was happing, he just didn't know how bad it was going to be.

When the time is right, I will call

Max got to the lab five minutes after David, "Did you get a hold of Barry?" He asked.

"No, he is not in his room, and he isn't answering his cell."

"He's probably down at the tables, if he is, his phone would be off."

"Yeah, that sounds like him," David said. "We can do it without him."

"Yeah," Max agreed.

When they got to the evidence room, the phone was still ringing. David got down the box, and tore it open.

He answered the phone, "Hello?"

"David." The familiar voice of The Spade replied.

"What do you want?" David asked.

"I want to play a little game."

"What kind of game?"

"A game like the one that led you to that fat pig of a cop."

"Where is the first phone?"

"Oh no," The Spade mocked. "This time you will be finding notes, and if you're not fast enough, they will be gone, and you will lose, *again*."

"Where is the first *note*?"

"On the east side of the MGM, and don't worry, it is under a weight, you can't lose the first clue."

"OK,"

"For a little encouragement, I'll leave you with this,"

David heard The Spade give the phone to someone crying, "David?"

It was Barry.

He was taking deep sobs in between words, from crying, "David?"

"Yeah Barry."

"David help me, there are horrible things..." He stopped.

"Barry?"

The Spade answered his call. "That should get things going." he said. "Tick-tock, tick-tock."

"You better not hurt him." David threatened.

"Tick-tock, tick-tock, tick-tock, you're running out of time, David."

"MGM right?"

There was a slight pause. "Tick-tock, tick-tock-time is running out David. Tick-tock, tick-tock..."

31

Follow
Instructions

Barry woke up in a daze. He felt like he had a wild night.

What happened last night?

As Barry's vision started to come into focus, he didn't recognize his surroundings.

Where am I?

Barry's vision cleared, and he remembered what had happened. *I was attacked.*

Barry strained against the ropes that were tied around his arms and legs. Nothing happened, they were tied tight. After a few minutes, he managed to get a look at the room he was in, the sights made his hair stand up.

It appeared to be some sort of torture chamber. In one corner Barry saw an open sarcophagus with metal spikes sticking out. He could see blood dripping off the tips of some- they had been used recently.

Barry's pulse raced.

He looked towards the middle of the room, and saw a lead boot on top of a chair. In front of the chair there was a smoking pile of coals.

Barry began to panic.

Barry glanced towards the final corner and saw a wooden table with ropes at each corner. Beside the table was the crank that pulled the ropes tight.

Barry started to hyperventilate.

A shadow covered Barry, "Good, you're awake."

Barry couldn't see the man's face but he could see a blonde ponytail protruding out the back.

Barry spoke in between breaths. "Wh...what d...do y...you want wi...wi...with me?"

The Spade spoke with a strong confident voice, "You are to be my example."

"Example of what?" Barry said, regaining his composure.

"To prove how powerful I really am. I have seen you, all of you, you all have your doubts of my power, my genius."

The Spade paused, "Your death shall be a great step in my procedure. You death will have reason."

Barry couldn't speak and the fear had returned ten fold.

The Spade took out a phone, "First, I need to make a little call to your friends."

It took almost half an hour for someone to pick up. The Spade was starting to get restless when David answered it, "David," he said into the phone.

Barry was trying to figure out what David was saying.

"I want to play a little game."

He waited for David to reply. "A game like the one that led you to that fat pig of a cop."

"Oh, no." The Spade said, "This time you will be finding notes, and if you are not fast enough, they will be gone, and you will lose, *again*."

Notes? Barry thought.

"On the east side of the MGM," Barry guessed that he was telling David where to start. "Don't worry it is under a weight, you can't lose the first clue."

"For a little encouragement I'll leave you with this."

The Spade leaned down and put the phone to Barry's ear, "David?"

"Yeah Barry."

"David help me, there are horrible things..." The Spade took the phone away.

"That should get things going," he said. "Tick-tock, tick-tock."

The Spade waited for a reply and then repeated himself. "Tick-tock, tick-tock, tick-tock, you are running out of time, David."

The Spade paused again. "Tick-tock, tick-tock-time is running out David. Tick-tock, tick-tock."

Then The Spade closed the phone, turned to Barry, and smiled, "Now the fun begins."

David stood breathless for a minute, Max broke him out of his trance. "David?"

"Yeah?"

"What about the notes?"

David started to explain, "He has Barry, he left us a trail of notes to find him."

"How much time do we have?"

"He didn't say, but very little," he paused. "The first note is on the east side of the MGM, let's get started."

They got to the MGM five minutes later, out of breath. "Wh...ere is the first note again?" Max asked catching his breath.

"He said on the east side of the MGM," David said, as they ran around to it. When they got to the part of the hotel that The Spade had told them about, they saw it almost instantly. It was sticking out from under a rock, weighted down like The Spade had said. Max ran over to

it, and lifted up the rock, revealing the note.
It was folded into a perfect square. Max picked
it up and unfolded it, revealing the first
clue.

You can listen.
You can stay.
Your next clue will blow away.

Max read it again and then handed it to
David.

The Spade picked Barry up and brought him
over to the lead boot.

"What are you doing?" Barry asked
trembling.

"Oh," The Spade, said in a mocking voice.
"You'll see, oh just wait."

He put Barry down on the chair and tied
him to the chair with another rope. The he went
down on his knees and untied one of his legs.
As soon as the rope was gone, Barry kicked The
Spade in the face as hard as he could. The
Spade, unprepared for this, flew back onto the
bed of coals. He jumped back up in surprise.

"Barry," said The Spade in an aggravated
voice. "That didn't improve your current
situation." He walked back up to Barry and
connected cleanly with Barry's jaw.

Barry screamed and spat out a bloody glob
with a tooth in it.

The Spade looked at him and smiled, "If
you think that hurt, wait till you wear the
boot."

Once again The Spade got to his knees and
lifted up Barry's leg. He then pulled the boot
towards him. He slipped Barry's foot into the
boot then he lifted it and dropped it into the
bed of coals.

At first Barry felt nothing, but then it
began. It started as a slight burn, like

standing too close to a fire. Then it started
to feel like a burn you got from holding a
match too long. Finally, it escalated to a
level of heat Barry had never felt before. It
was unbearable. Barry screamed in agony.

"Let's stop that screaming now." The Spade
said, putting tape over his mouth.

Barry tried to scream through the tape,
but it muffled it out.

The Spade smiled, "Just wait until I show
you the rest of the room."

"You can listen, you can stay, your next
clue will blow away." Max read again. "What
does that mean?"

"Well if is like the last trail, the next
clue is at a hotel."

"You can listen, you can stay," David
whispered to himself again trying to make sense
of the clue. "That could mean anything."

"Wait," Max said. "Maybe we are trying too
hard to figure this out."

David was confused.

"Let's just slow down and think logically,
the name of the hotel might mean something."

"You can listen, you can stay." Max said.
"What hotels could mean that?"

David suddenly understood, "It's the Rio."

"What?" Max said. "How did you figure it
out?"

"Think about it," David started to explain
to him. "You can stay, meaning the hotel."

"*Yeah*," Max said annoyed. "I knew that
part had to be a hotel, but what does the "you
can listen" mean?"

"I was in Best Buy last month, looking at
MP3 players and one of them was a Rio."

"You can listen." Max suddenly got it too.
"Like the MP3 you can listen to it."

"Yep," David said then focused on the other part of the clue. "Your next clue will blow away."

"Just as was I thinking, we better get going."

When they got to the Rio, they were in a panic. They had no idea where to look this time, and if it took too long, they would lose this clue and/or the others, however many there were. They split up, and scanned the sides of the hotel. They met in the middle five minutes later, with nothing.

"Shit," Max said. "We have to look harder, and faster."

They switched sides and continued to look. On the second go around David saw it. The note was folded into a square like the first, and it was blowing towards the road

Your next clue will blow away.

David chased after it as the note blew into the path of a car. David dove into the road, and grabbed the note with one hand. He turned around to headlights and a blasting horn. David jumped back into the grass at the last second.

The man rolled down his window, he had a deep New Yorker accent, "Hey buddy, what the hell's your problem?"

David just ignored him, and walked back towards Max.

"What's it say?" Max asked.

David opened the second clue.

An ancient tomb holds your next clue.
Better hurry before it comes unglued.

Just when Barry thought that he was going to pass out the pain stopped. He opened his eyes to see The Spade had put out the coals, and doused the boot in water.

Barry let out a sigh of relief.

The Spade looked over and gave that menacing grin of his again, "Why don't we stretch out those muscles a little bit?"

The Spade tapped the boot a few times with the edge hand to make sure it was cooled down. When he was sure it did, he took it off Barry's foot, "Oh, that looks good."

Barry glanced down at his foot, it was a mess. His foot was charred black, and the blisters on it were oozing blood. He looked back up at The Spade with a look of hopelessness.

"Oh," The Spade punched his foot, sending a wave of pain through his entire body. "Calm down now, the fun has just begun."

The Spade picked up Barry and brought him over to the table. He laid him down and untied his other leg, this time Barry made no effort to struggle, there was no use, he was clearly overpowered now. After he tied Barry up, The Spade went to the other side, and began turning the wheel. Like the boot, the pain started dully, almost enough to annoy you, then it grew. Barry winced as he was stretched further, and further. Right when Barry thought that all of his joints were going to pop out, The Spade stopped turning the wheel.

Barry turned to look around. *It can't be over*.

When The Spade came back into view, he couldn't hold back his scream.

"An ancient tomb holds your next clue, better hurry before it comes unglued," David said. "The first part is easy, the hotel is the Luxor, but what is the part about coming unglued?"

"How do you know it is the Luxor?" Max asked.

"Think about it, the Luxor has a giant pyramid at the entrance, pyramids are where pharaohs were buried when they died, an ancient tomb." David explained.

Max nodded in agreement, "I see now."

Five minutes later they were standing at the entrance of the Luxor.

Max repeated the second line of the clue again. "Better hurry before it comes unglued."

"What can that mean?"

David thought about it for a minute. "Maybe it is somewhere where it will be destroyed if it falls."

"Yeah," Max agreed. "But where could it be, I don't think he would put it inside, where could it be out here that it would be destroyed if it came unglued?"

"*Maybe*," David said. "We are over thinking this again, there is a pretty high wind tonight, maybe he is referring to it coming unglued and blowing away."

"That does make sense," Max said. "He loves to play mind games. It might be glued to the outside of the pyramid."

David got the entire clue, "That's it, an ancient tomb *holds* your next clue."

"Let's search the perimeter again," Max said.

They found the clue on their first go around. The problem was that it was out of reach. Max spotted it first, and pointed it out to David. The note was glued about twelve feet above the ground.

"Shit," David said when Max showed him. "How the hell are we supposed to get that?"

"I don't know," Max said, looking up at the note that was starting to flap in the wind a little. "But we better find out fast, or Barry is gone."

A thought suddenly came to David; it

seemed a little foolish, and a bit dangerous, "Why don't you just hoist me up and I will grab it?"

Max thought for a minute. "Alright." He got down on his knees and put his hands together. "Hop up."

David stepped on Max's hand and jumped at the same time Max hoisted, David came just out of reach of the clue.

"Damn," David said.

Max got back down. "Let's try again."

This time he was able to grab it.

David came back down with the third clue.

Our First President called this home.

Your final clue is at the top of the climb.

Barry continued to scream through the tape as The Spade came towards him with a glowing red brand. It was small and circular; Barry couldn't make out the design in the middle. The Spade leaned over Barry's head and brushed back his hair.

Barry knew instantly what was about to happen.

The Spade saw the fear in his eyes and smiled. Then he pushed down the brand. Barry screamed in pain as he smelled his burning flesh for the second time today.

The Spade lifted the brand, happy with his work.

"Where to next?" The Spade said. "Should I just get it over with and put you in your grave." he motioned over to the sarcophagus in the corner. "Or should I go find another method?"

Barry looked up at him with tears in his eyes.

"Oh," The Spade said joyfully. "Why let the fun stop? Let me see what else I can find for you."

With that The Spade left, leaving Barry
alone.

Fifteen minutes later The Spade walked
back into the room. To Barry each minute had
seemed like an eternity. He had prayed to God
someone would find him, someone would smell him
burning, but no one did. The Spade had him
somewhere where no one could help him. He was
doomed.

When the door first opened, Barry was
filled with joy, he thought it was someone
coming to rescue him. His joy melted into fear
when he saw the familiar cowboy outfit of The
Spade. He leaned over to see what The Spade had
found to torture him with. He saw The Spade had
a fish tank and a bag of groceries.

What? Barry thought. *What's he going to do
with those?*

Barry watched as The Spade put the fish
tank on the ground and started to unload the
bag. First he took out a bottle of syrup.

Barry continued to wonder what The Spade
was going to do to him.

The next thing The Spade took out of the
bag made everything make sense. The Spade
pulled out an ant farm. He walked back over to
Barry, tied his legs back together then retied
his arms. When he was sure that Barry was
securely tied back up, The Spade cut the ropes
that were stretching him out. He then lifted
Barry and put him on the chair, then he brought
over the fish tank. He lifted up Barry's feet,
and dropped them in. The Spade went back and
got the syrup and the ant farm. First, he
poured the entire bottle of syrup on Barry's
feet. Then he lifted up the ant farm, and
dumped it in the tank. Barry could feel the
ants moving around.

The Spade was laughing, "The bite of a

fire ant can be harmless, but a whole army can kill you."

Barry watched as they began to crawl up his legs. When they reached his knees they bit. It seemed that they waited until they were all there before they bit.

The bite of a fire ant can be harmless, but a whole army can kill you.

"Our First President called this home, your next clue is at the top of the climb," Max said.

"Our first president?" David said. "What does George Washington have to do with Vegas?"

"He called it home," Max repeated. "Is there anything here that has to do with DC?" Max said.

"No, I don't think so," David said. "Maybe the second line will help us more."

"Doubt it," Max said. "Your next clue is at the top of the climb. That sounds like *where* in the hotel it is."

"Washington DC, Washington DC," David was saying. "Wash..."

"...ington DC," Max finished. "It is named after him."

"Yeah," David said. "So?"

"He couldn't have lived there when he was president," Max said. "We have been trying too hard again. I remember now, he was the only president not to live in the White House. When he was selected as president the capital of the United States was New York."

"The New York, New York," David said.

"Yep," Max said. "Which if my memory serves me well it has a roller costar on the roof."

"Your next clue is at the top of the climb," David said. "We'd better go."

When they got to the New York, New York, they ran right up to the roof. When they reached it, they stood face to face with a mile long line.

"Shit," Max said. "What are we going to do now?"

David took out his badge, "That's where these babies come in handy."

They ran to the front of the line, passing many disgruntled people, who made no attempt to hide their anger.

When they got to the front of the line, they saw the clue. It was being blown against the podium that the ride supervisor was standing at. It looked like a napkin, so no one gave it a second look.

Max went over to pick it up, "Good thing no one here cares about litter."

He opened the final clue and groaned.

Go back to where your quest began.
In room 312 you will find your man.

The pain from the bites was excruciating, especially on the foot that had been burned. Again, just when the pain was going to knock him out, The Spade relieved him. He sprayed the tank with a fire extinguisher, killing the ants. The Spade just stood there for a moment, watching Barry.

"Take the next five minutes to think about your life, and make your final prayers to God, you'll be with him soon," The Spade said, as he went over to the sarcophagus and twisted a hook in the ceiling right in between the door and the spikes. Then he came back and stood by Barry, giving him his five.

When the time was up, The Spade picked him up and brought him to his final toy of torture. He lifted him up and hung him by his wrists.

"You have ten minutes," The Spade said. "Ten minutes until your coffin snaps shut. Do you trust that your colleagues will find you in time?" The Spade set up a timer. "Let's see."

Barry started to cry.

The Spade tipped his hat. "I bid you adieu."

Then he left.

"Shit!" David yelled. "Shit, shit, shit! He sent us on a meaningless trail, only to lead us back to where we started."

"He needed more time," Max said.

"I know, he probably already killed Barry."

"Let's keep things positive," Max said. "We still have a chance."

"Yeah, you're right." David agreed.

When they got to the MGM, it had been an hour from the time they got the first call. The room key was fairly easy to obtain, once they showed their badges and explained the situation. They ran up to the room and opened the door.

Max and David were shocked at the contents of the room. It was a torture chamber, and in the far corner of the room, Barry hung in front of a coffin with spikes sticking out.

"Barry!" Max yelled, running over to him.

Max grabbed the chair in front of the coals and brought it over. He got up and unhooked Barry. Then he took the tape off Barry's mouth, and untied him.

Barry hugged Max, crying.

"Barry, it's alright, we're here, everything is going to be fine."

But like an overtired baby, Barry was beyond consoling.

32

The Sp♠de

When Barry woke up again, he was in the hospital. He glanced around and saw Max and David standing out in the hall, talking to a doctor.

Barry tried to call out to them, but his throat was drier than sand, and all that came out was a low moan. Barry had a vague recollection of what had happened. He remembered that he had been taken hostage, and there had been some horrible things done to him. He looked down at the edge of his bed, one of his feet was bigger than the other.

That boot thing, and the ant bites.

He tried to rub his head, there was an uncomfortable squeeze on it, like wearing a hat that was too small. What he felt shocked him, there was a bandage wrapped tightly around the top of his head.

What the hell?

Then he remembered the table, how he thought that his arms and legs were going to be pulled out, only to realize that the outcome was going to be much worse. The Spade had branded him, you could pop back in bones, but you can't get rid of a brand, he was now permanently marked by him.

Five minutes later, the doctor walked in with Max and David. He walked over to Barry and held out his hand.

"Hello, I'm Dr. Wilson, how are you feeling?"

Barry tired to talk again, but like the first time, only a low moan escaped his mouth.

The doctor instantly knew what was wrong, he reached over to his side table and picked up a glass of water. He bent the straw down towards Barry.

Barry took a long drink of water, "I'm still a little out of it."

"I would bet you are," he replied. "I am surprised that you have regained consciousness so fast, by the amount of poison that is in your body."

"Oh," Barry said. "how much?"

"A lot," he said. "If they had not gotten to you when they did," he motioned over to Max and David. "It might have killed you."

"Was it enough to make me..."

Dr. Wilson finished the sentence for him. "Allergic? Yes, I recommend that when you get out, you carry this with you at *all* times." He put an epinephrine on the table by Barry's table. "Another bite might kill you."

"And what about my...my um, head?" Barry asked almost afraid to hear the answer.

"Well the thing with that is," the doctor paused. "How can I put this in perspective? You..."

David got tired of the doctor pretending that what had happened to Barry's head was *so* medically complicated, "He branded you, Barry."

"Yeah," Barry replied. "I remember that, but what...what did he brand me with?"

"Do you remember Dominic?" Max said. "What was on his back?"

Barry saw where this was going, and blamed himself for not knowing better, "Yeah."

"Same thing on your head," David explained. "Except it has a figure in the middle."

"A figure?"

"Yeah." Max said.

"What does it look like?"

"Kind of like a diamond with two arms." Max replied.

"What?" Barry said surprised. "What does that mean?"

"We have no idea." Max said.

"Well," Barry said. "When can I see it?"

"As soon as it heals up a little," the doctor said. "Which should be in a few days."

"Alright," Barry answered.

"And I think that Mr. Johnson should get some more rest, could you please leave?"

David and Max looked a little mad, but they didn't feel like arguing. "Bye Barry," Max and David said.

"Bye guys," Barry said, then he turned towards the wall, and drifted off again.

The next day when Barry was getting the dead skin removed off his leg, he wished he was still knocked out. The pain was almost as bad as the pain he had suffered while wearing the boot, and to make things worse, they kept pulling off the scabs left by the ants. He winced and pushed his head into the pillow, wishing for the pain to finally end.

The next week, Barry got his wish. They had stopped scrubbing the dead skin off, and had cleared him for release. Before he left he asked the doctor to take off the bandage around his head. The doctor agreed, and began unwrapping the bandage. Barry felt a kind of excitement that he assumed people felt after they had plastic surgery. He stared at the mirror watching as layer, after layer, after layer was removed. Unlike plastic surgeries though, Barry was not pleased to see what was under the bandages.

The brand was a spade with a symbol inside that looked a diamond with arms.

Barry stared at the brand for a moment, trying to figure out what it meant. His first impression was that it was another Greek symbol, but it didn't look like anything he recognized from that book. That didn't mean anything though, Barry had never been a foreign language scholar. After a few minutes, Barry got up, and left. Max and David were waiting for him outside.

"Hey Barry." Max said.

"How are you feeling?" David asked as they were getting into the car.

"I am felling better, but..."

"What?" Max asked.

Barry lifted up his bangs reveling the brand.

"*Oh*," Max said, like he was in pain. "I see."

"What else happened?" David said.

"Well, I got the skin rubbed off my leg for the last four days, and now I'm allergic to ants."

"That sounds like fun," David said sarcastically.

"Don't even start," Barry said, in a stern voice.

"We were going to go back to the room, and see if we can find anything that can lead us to the killer."

"By the way," Max said. "Did you get a good look at him?"

"No," Barry said. "He had on that cowboy outfit, and the lights were low."

"Did you see the color of his eyes?"

"I think they were brown, or blue, like I said the lights were low and I could not get a good look at him."

Max and David looked a little mad, but they didn't say anything.

They got back to the MGM at about three o'clock. When they went up to the room, all the memories of that night came flooding back. Barry looked around, suddenly feeling uneasy. He walked around and looked at the devices that had made him want to die. The sick feeling had disappeared; in its place was a level of rage that Barry had never felt before. He picked up the chair that had held the boot, and went over to the table, ready to smash it. Luckily, David saw him and before he could smash the chair, he pulled it away from him. "Barry," David said sternly. "You have to control yourself." He put the chair back near the cooled down coals. "Now, will you be able to do that?"

Barry took a deep breath, and told the truth, "No, I don't think I can, not yet at least."

"OK," David said. "That's perfectly fine. You can go back to the lab. We pulled the security tapes from the parking lot. Can you go and look at them, you are like Max when it comes to noticing little details."

"Yeah, sure," Barry said, as he walked out of the room. "I will see you guys later."

Barry got to the lab at three thirty. He went in and popped in the tapes. The first tape showed nothing. Barry could hardly even see the car. All he could see was the back end of the car blowing up. No suspect or anything else that showed anything new. Barry sighed, and popped in the next tape.

Max and David were processing the room when they found it. David was looking at the spikes coming out of the sarcophagus. He tried to chip off some of the blood, but to his surprise the blood was still wet.

"Hey Max, you might want to come take a look at this."

Max came over from the coals, "What is it?"

"This blood is still wet."

"What?" Max said surprised. "That's impossible."

"Look," David took out a swab, and brushed it across a spike."

Max look at the swab. "What the...?" He took the swab and sniffed it. "Yep, that's what I thought."

Now David was the one in shock, "What?"

He handed the swab back to David, "It's paint."

David sniffed it, "But how is it still wet?"

"I don't remember exactly how it works, but if you mix oil with paint, it never dries."

"Yeah," David agreed. "I think I saw that on CSI."

Max went back to the chair as David bagged the swab. As he was sealing the bag, he dropped it.

David sighed and bent down to pick it up. It was then that he saw the piece of paper sticking out from under the sarcophagus.

David instantly knew what it was. "Max, I think there is another note."

"Where?"

"Under the sarcophagus," David said, as Max came back over.

"Do you think that you can lift it enough for me to grab it?"

"Yeah," Max said. "I can try."

Max got a good grip near the bottom, and heaved. The sarcophagus flipped forward and collapsed.

"Shit," David said walking over to it. "its made of cardboard-the whole thing was a joke-he never intended to kill him."

"Well lets look at what he left us." Max said.

They unwrapped the new note.
One more clue to go.
And you will have me on death row.
The last clue is not far.
In the front of the great India Temple.

Barry stared intently at the second tape, looking for anything out of the ordinary. This next tape showed a little more of the parking lot than the first. He could see all of the cars and people walking around. Barry looked at the time; it was ten minutes before the blast. Barry started to fast forward it, when he saw what he was looking for. He rewound it and played it again in slow motion. He saw it again, his eyes were not playing tricks on him. Barry watched as someone walked by, and put something on the bottom of the car. Then he saw the man pull out a controller and push a button twice, arming the bomb. Barry started to get the last tape ready, to see if it revealed anything else.

"The great India Temple?" Max said. "What do you get from that?"

"I don't know," David said. "It has to be some sort of hotel, or maybe a store."

Max put the note in his pocket, "The first part of the clue is what intrigues me the most," he said. "One more clue to go, and you will have me on death row. It's like he's giving up, turning himself in."

"Well," David said. "We thought he was doing that when we were at the last scene. Remember how much evidence we found?"

"Yeah," Max said. "We were right, he wants to be caught, he wants the publicity."

"So," Max said, going back to the clue. "Where could this lead us?"

"Well," David said. "We need to figure out what the India Temple means first. Is it a direct reference, or is it a type of word game like the clue that led us to the Rio."

"I don't know."

"Why don't we make this a little easier," David said. "Let's just name all the hotels; one of them might fit the clue."

"Alright," Max said. "MGM, Rio, Bellagio."

"No," David said, as he named some. "New York New York, Luxor, the Trump..."

David stopped.

"David?"

David had figured it out again, "The Trump Taj Mahal."

"Ah, I should have gotten that," Max said. "The great India Temple, it's so obvious."

When they got to the Taj Mahal, it was quarter to five. They ran up and looked in all the usual places where the note would be. To their surprise, it was under a stone, like the first at the MGM. Max lifted up the rock, and read the final clue.

Congratulations on making it this far.
Give the desk clerk your name and go to the top.

Barry was getting the final tape ready, when his cell phone rang, "Hello?"

"Barry, it's David."

"Hey, what's happened with the case?"

"We just found the final clue, we are about to catch him. He is at the Taj Mahal."

"Great," Barry said. "So, it's over?"

"Yeah," David said. "It's about to end."

Barry hung up. "It's over," he said to himself.

He looked at the tape in his hands, "What the hell?" he said as he popped it in.

Barry stared at the familiar scene of the parking lot. He watched as the suspect got in, and then the blast came. Barry stopped, and rewound it. Did he see what he thought he saw? He played it again, and saw the same thing.

"Oh my God," Barry said, as he grabbed his keys and ran out the door.

"Well let's do what it says." Max said, as he pocketed the final clue. "Let's give the desk clerks our name."

They walked in, and went over to the front desk.

The lady at the front desk smiled at them, "Can I help you?"

"Yeah," Max said. "Do you have a message for a Max Levin-ton?"

"Let me check." She turned around and flipped through, some papers. "No sorry, do you have the right hotel?"

"Yeah," Max said disappointed. "Thanks."
"Wait," David stepped up. "Do you have a message for a David Walker?"

The lady went back to the papers, and shuffled through them. She came back with an envelope, "Yeah, I do, but I need to see some ID first."

David showed her.

"Thank you." She handed him the envelope. "Have a good day."

"You too," David said, as he walked back towards Max.

He opened the envelope and a key fell out. David picked it up and inspected it, "Go to the top," David said.

"What?"

"This is a key to the penthouse. Go to the top."

"Let's go."

David went with Max to the elevator that would take them to their final destination.

Before they walked in they drew their guns. The penthouse was very nice, but it seemed deserted.

The drapes were pulled shut, blocking out the light.

"Shit," Max said. "This looks like a dead end."

"He got us again," David said.

They turned around to go back to the elevator when the power went out.

"Max?" David yelled into the darkness.

There was no answer.

"Max?" David called again.

This time a blood chilling scream met his call.

"Max!"

David felt his way around the room, trying to find Max.

"Ma..." David stopped as he felt the knife enter his chest.

His put his hand on his chest as the knife went in and out. David fell to the ground, knowing he was going to die.

As he was sitting there, he felt someone standing over him, "It's over," he heard a familiar voice whisper.

Then, the pain stopped.

At five twenty, Barry arrived at the hotel. He got out of his car and saw Max walking out of the hotel.

"Where's David?"

"You just missed him," Max said, as he was walking towards him, he took The Spade down to the station."

"Why are you here?"

"I was waiting for you, so we could process his room; see if we can find anything that will help catch his partner or partners."

"Oh."

Max walked towards him, "I actually found something you might find interesting."

"Really?"

"Yeah," Max walked towards Barry. "Look."

Barry knew he might try something like this, and he was ready when the knife came at him. Barry caught Max's hand and broke his arm with one solid chop. Max screamed in pain, and tried to swipe at him again. Barry caught Max's hand and flipped him on his back. Max looked at Barry in shock, gasping for breath. Barry jumped on top of him, "By the way, I have something you might find interesting too," Barry slapped cuffs on him. "I'm a third degree black belt."

Epilogue: The Complexity of Perfection

Barry took Max's knife and gun, and put them by his side. He pointed the gun at Max, "I should kill you right now, you miserable piece of shit." Barry looked up towards the sound of the nearing sirens. "But I'm not like you." Barry put down the gun, and flagged down the police cars.

The police lifted Max up, and read him his rights as they put him in the back of a cruiser.

A week before his trail, Barry visited Max in his holding cell.

"Why did you do it?" Barry asked.

"You mean you haven't figured it out yet?" Max said. "*You* the amazing detective phenonm."

"No," Barry admitted. "I want to know your motive."

"Think about it, Barry," Max said. "Think about the names of the victims."

Barry thought about it, "What about the names? They are completely random."

Max sat up, "I know, that's the beauty of it."

"What?"

"It seems like every killing was random, in that way we achieved perfection."

"The killings weren't random?"

"Yes the killings were, but every name had meaning."

Barry was still confused, and Max saw it

in his face.

"Think about it, Logan and Ann, Rob and Denise, Chief *Victor* Powell. Setting off any alarms yet?"

"No."

"Eddie, Dominic, Andy, and Ken?"

Barry was still confused.

"WALTER AND IVA!!" Max yelled.

"I don't get it."

"Think," Max pointed to his head. "Think about the names. Do the letters mean anything to you?"

"Well," Barry thought for a little, and then he got it. "My, God."

Max smiled. "Yes, he finally gets it."

"The first letters of all the names spell out 'David Walker'. This whole thing was about him, only about him."

"Yes, that was the whole plan."

"But, why?"

"Revenge."

"For what?"

"Do you remember that whole thing about me tampering with evidence, and taking payoffs from major criminals?"

"Ye…" Barry stopped. "It was all true?"

"Every bit of it, and David ruined it."

"So you killed him, and eleven other innocent people."

"Thirteen."

"Excuse me?"

"Thirteen, we killed thirteen."

"How?"

"Well, do you remember in *Silence of the Lambs* when Hannibal made that guy swallow his own tongue? Well that is what we managed to do to Richard. We drove him to death through clever manipulation."

"And the thirteenth?"

"Well Joe could have saved himself."

"How?"

"Did you hear about how I was stabbed when this case first opened?"

"Yeah I read that somewhere."

"I met up with him, to destroy the evidence. He was supposed to just take it, and I was going to say that I was held up at gun point. Then when it happened he stabbed me, leaving me to die."

"But you didn't."

"Nope, and as soon as I got out of the hospital, his death warrant was signed, he just didn't know it."

"Surely he knew that you would want revenge?"

"Nope, I told him that he just panicked, and I would have done the same thing if I was in his shoes."

"And he believed you?" Barry said in shock.

"Sure, we both had a lot to lose if we got caught."

"What was he going to lose?"

"You saw his rap sheet, we had enough on him to lock him up and throw away the key. I kept him safe, and out of the law's hands."

"Oh."

"Which leads us to that pesky little brand."

Barry touched his forehead. "What does it mean?"

"Well for one, it's not a Greek symbol. It's a number."

"Which one?"

"It's a combination of X and V. Basically, fifteen."

"Fifteen?"

"Yes, you were supposed to be the fifteenth and final victim that night in the parking lot, but you figured me out. How did you do that?"

"Basic human reflexes."

"What did I do?"

"In the parking lot, you ducked right before the bomb went off."

Max's face went white, "So one little *fucking* mistake ruined all my hard work?"

"Hard work-what hard work?"

"Do you know how hard it was for me to play stupid? To pretend like I had no idea what was going on. To have my associate give me a note to make it look like they were after me? Actually, it was amusing to me near the end. I choose my words carefully to let them know it was me. But, no one figured it out-no one."

"If that's what you call it, then yes," Barry said as he left, he had all he needed.

"Wait." Max called out. "Do you want to know who they are-who my associates are."

"Really?"

"Sure, they are all gone anyway. It was Ryan, I am lucky that you did not remember the ponytail."

Barry gasped, it did go up far, "And the female."

"The role of the female goes to the beautiful Mrs. Levinton." Max said clapping.

Barry began to walk away as Max called out, "It's not over. Wait until the ending. You are going to love the ending."

Max stood facing the judge, "Maxwell Levinton," she said. "You are accused of fourteen counts of first degree murder, as well as one count of attempted murder in the first degree. How do you plea?"

Max looked her straight in the face, "Guilty, your honor."

His lawyer stood up and whispered to him and then turned to the judge. "Your honor, let me have a moment with my client."

"As you wish."

Max and his lawyer stood congregating for a few moments when Max leaned over and whispered something in his lawyer's ear. His face went ghost white, and then he grabbed his suitcase and ran out of the court.

"What was that about?"

Max turned back to the judge, "I told him that his wife was much more beautiful before she dyed her hair blonde."

"Excuse me?"

"Then I told him that if he wants the brown to grow back, he better get back home before my buddy finds out that this arraignment is lasting too long."

"O...ok."

"Now as I said, I plead guilty."

"Are you sure?"

Max stared at the judge.

The judge got the picture, "Alright, the sentencing will take place in two weeks." She banged her gavel. "Court is adjourned."

Two weeks later, Max got the death penalty, "Do you want to appeal?"

"No," Max said. "Kill me, release me from *this* life."

Almost a year later, after numerous piles of paperwork to deny any appeals, Max finally got his date. Barry came back from New York for the execution. They gave him a front row seat. Barry watched as they got him ready. They strapped him into the chair, and lowered a microphone.

"Maxwell Levinton, you have been sentenced to die by lethal injection. Do you have any last words?"

Barry leaned forward. Max spoke the words

slowly, the words made Barry's blood run cold,
"It has only be*gun*,"

No sooner had those four words escaped
Max's cold lips, the power went out.

"What the hell?" the guards said.

Barry started to panic.

There was a loud crash, and the vent above
Max popped open.

In the dark Barry could make out ropes
coming down. Three soldiers came down with
machine guns and flashlights, one of them had a
blonde ponytail. They opened fire and killed
all the guards. Barry watched in horror as they
unstrapped Max. Max leaned up and kissed the
smallest solider. Then he walked over to the
window, and breathed on it. It the fog, Max
drew a Spade.

Then he backed up, gave a salute to the
crowd, and disappeared up the vent.

September 9, 2003-May 20, 2007 RJP

www.ingramcontent.com/pod-product-compliance
Lightning Source LLC
Chambersburg PA
CBHW032028240626
47154CB00003B/831